WATER BOUND

WATER BOUND

DRAGON OF SHADOW AND AIR BOOK SEVEN

JESS MOUNTIFIELD

DISRUPTIVE IMAGINATION

THE WATER BOUND TEAM

Thanks to our JIT Team:

Diane L. Smith
Dave Hicks
Deb Mader
Dorothy Lloyd
Jeff Goode

If We've missed anyone, please let us know!

Editor
SkyHunter Editing Team

LMBPN Publishing supports the right to free expression and the value of copyright. The purpose of copyright is to encourage writers and artists to produce the creative works that enrich our culture.

The distribution of this book without permission is a theft of the author's intellectual property. If you would like permission to use material from the book (other than for review purposes), please contact support@lmbpn.com. Thank you for your support of the author's rights.

LMBPN Publishing
PMB 196, 2540 South Maryland Pkwy
Las Vegas, NV 89109

Version 1.01 September 2021
eBook ISBN: 978-1-68500-436-1
Print ISBN: 978-1-68500-437-8

Dedication:

To Bryan. For holding my hand in the dark.

CHAPTER ONE

The beach stretched out before Zephyr and me. The sun was setting and turning the water a beautiful orange. It was one of the first times we'd had a chance to come down to the sand during the day since Jacobs had been arrested and we'd been pardoned.

Over two months had passed, and we'd been busy with the aftermath. The LAPD had wanted our input on policing mythicals, and we'd officially signed on for training. Crawley had taken over the agency to help with that, but she had a good idea of how to handle things.

On top of that, the Sanctuary was in negotiations with the US over owning their lands and governing themselves.

And Zephyr and I had grown closer. His human form was a part of him I'd not only grown used to but appreciated in more ways than one.

Right now, he was beside me in dragon form. The face he took in human form we still kept a secret as far as we could. I leaned against him, Sen sitting on my lap, and tried to think of something better than this. There wasn't much.

We should do some training, or Minsheng won't be happy when we get back, Zephyr sent.

I sighed and got to my feet. Zephyr did the same a moment later, and I noticed people staring and pointing at us. Despite the media focus we'd had and how general public opinion had swung to being supportive, there were still a fair few people who were scared of us.

It will be worse when they're not. Zephyr shook, spraying sand and making me blast it down with air to stop myself from getting covered. *They'll mob us everywhere we go.*

I'm sure they won't, I replied. *And if they try, I can use my abilities to form a barrier around us and keep them out.*

Or I could fly us to a quieter section of beach.

This is LA. There is no quieter section of the beach at this time of day.

There is if it's raining, Zephyr replied, huffing as he threw his head to one side.

I fought a chuckle, pretty sure he wasn't serious. Training in the rain didn't sound fun either, despite me trying to take control of water.

That was why we were on the beach.

Concentrating, I reached for the air and sent it around in circles, getting a feel for the way I could use it without doing anything major with it. I then did the same with the sand, feeling it and the seaweed, algae, and other living plant life among it, on it, and in the water. It felt very different from the air, but I reached out and took control of it.

More than once, Emily and Gwaelon had told me water felt different, possibly because living beings contained so much liquid. Both had described it as becoming one with the water and guiding it in a very strange way.

However it was done, they thought I ought to be capable of it. Gwaelon was pretty sure I'd managed at least *some* control in the past. While I wasn't going to argue with him, I wasn't convinced. This was hard.

As when I'd tried before, nothing seemed to happen. I didn't feel at one with the waves in front of me, nor did the ocean listen to my thoughts. The sea continued to be the sea as if I weren't standing in front of it.

I sighed and shook my head. Although the Sanctuary, the organization, and Minsheng believed I was going to be able to control four elements, I still wasn't sure they were right.

You will be able to do this, Zephyr said. *Let's try again later. Erlan and the others are here. Having Emily around might help.*

Wondering how Zephyr had sensed the other mythicals when we were still several hundred meters from them, I turned to greet them and hid my futile attempt to control the water.

Emily was the first to come over to me; she was the half-elf I'd rescued the previous year. With her were a few of the elves we'd rescued from an agency lab a short while later: Erlan with Newton on his shoulder and Ascan.

Ascan and Emily were water elves, and thankfully both of them had enough experience to help me teach the others. I noticed Jinto had come with them. He was officially Ascan's Shishou, but since we had a lot more elves in our group than the organization had Shishous close by, I was doing a lot of the teaching.

"Minsheng said he had some business with the dwarves

stationed nearby and that he didn't think you needed him anymore anyway," Jinto said, smiling. "How's the training coming along?"

Remembering how wary Minsheng had been in front of the other Shishou when we'd met and how he'd deliberately encouraged me to keep the full extent of my abilities a secret, I merely gave the man a slight bow.

"It's progressing, but as always, there are plenty of new tricks and combinations to learn," I replied, before shifting my focus to the rest of the group. It was a non-answer, but I had more important things to focus on.

We'd deliberately moved one of our training sessions a week to the beach. Partially because it provided a different environment to practice in and partially because it allowed normal humans a chance to see what we were capable of, but also see us using our abilities for useful purposes and calm, controlled beauty.

With that in mind, I encouraged the earth elementals to start sculpting the sand and playing with it. At the same time, I lifted a bunch of metal fire pits off the truck Jinto had used to get everyone there. With my air control, I could lift most things without trouble, and it was a simple way I could set up my classes.

With the fire pits in place, the earth elementals creating something together, and the water elementals under the guidance of Emily, who was trying to direct the flow of the water to fill a moat farther up the beach, I only had the air elementals to worry about.

I stirred up the air around them and sent it in a loop, my control on it looser than normal but still something they'd be aware of. There didn't need to be a conversation between us for them to start challenging me for control of the air particles or to have the wind that was rushing around them answer to them instead of me.

Although the other elves had varying strengths of will, I found the task easy. The group quickly gave up, instead having the strongest of them form her loop and the rest battle with her.

Overseeing the groups but no longer needed by the air elves, I was free to move closer to Emily and Ascan and see if there was something I had missed. While I had the chance, I wanted to try to learn as well.

Emily flicked me a grin as she batted the water down a sand channel so fast it knocked a chunk off the sculpture and made an earth elemental sigh.

Feeling sorry for the earth elemental and remembering how difficult it had been to do anything in the early days, I reached out for the earth and repaired the structure, pulling sand from elsewhere and making it denser.

If I didn't know any better, I'd say you're showing off, Zephyr said. Sen bounded off my shoulder and across the sand.

The small dryad-based myconid was the other mythical I was bonded to, and she enjoyed playing in the water and running around the beach. She'd grown up in a forest, and we'd come across each other many months earlier.

I moved closer to Sen as she darted up to a wave, and before I knew it, I was standing beside Emily, with Sen running around in the edge of the water. The myconid had to be careful since she was so small, but she loved the thrill of facing the danger the water represented to her.

Not that I was worried she'd drown. She could float

and bob to the surface quickly before rolling herself onto her back, but I didn't want to lose her.

Emily turned to me, still smiling.

"Thank you," she said. "For everything you've done for our kind. I've never felt so free to be myself. And Mother loves her new job."

I grinned back, grateful she was so happy. I'd worried about her at first. She'd been through a lot before I'd rescued her, and she'd barely understood her powers.

"How is it going with controlling water?" she asked a moment later.

"Not well," I replied, deciding to be honest. "I can't work out how it's different from the other two elements."

Emily studied me for a moment before looking at the water and then at me.

"Are you okay with getting wet?" she asked. "I think I could probably dry you out afterward, but I'm still working on that trick."

I lifted an eyebrow but decided to trust the young elf. After all, she had recently learned to control water. If anyone could help me, she was a good bet.

Taking my hand, she strode into the waves with me. Sen immediately bounded onto my shoulder, bringing water with her and splashing me.

The water felt cold at first, my body adjusting for a moment, but I didn't hesitate as Emily led me to where we were up to our waists.

"Close your eyes and feel the water around you, the same way you do the air," she said.

I wasn't sure what she meant, but I closed my eyes. A moment later, I reached out to the air and moved it around above the water. Then I tried to reach for the waves, but nothing happened except that I was buffeted by yet another wave as it broke over me.

The coldness made me shiver. I almost gave up then and there, but Emily reached for my hand and placed it in the water with hers. I felt it swirling around my hand, seeming to brush against me.

Not sure what I was feeling, I tried to work out where the water was moving and in what pattern against my hand. It felt as if Emily might be controlling it, and I reached deeper into the water, feeling her connection in the atoms.

As I did, I realized why it felt so strange having the water brush against me. It didn't feel as if I were being caressed by water, but instead, like it was her skin touching mine. The water she was in control of felt like her.

No sooner had I thought this than I remembered how she said she'd felt the first time she'd controlled liquids. Emily said she'd been carrying drinks, and it had felt as if she'd become them. I'd thought she'd meant something very different, but it was clear I'd been thinking about it wrong.

This time as I reached out to control the element, I tried to imagine it feeling like me, as if it were going to become an extension of my body. I placed my other hand in the water and reached downward and to the side.

At first nothing appeared to happen, but suddenly the connection came to life. My mind exploded with information about what the temperature was, what microorganisms were present, and the level of pollution.

I opened my eyes in shock. Every molecule of the water

around me was suddenly in my reach, and I was able to move it.

Controlling it drained me almost instantly as I stopped the waves from rushing against me, making the ocean accommodate my presence. The feeling scared me enough that I let go and took several steps back.

"Whoa! That *is* different."

"Isn't it? Fun though."

I frowned, not sure I'd have called it fun, but intrigued and wanting to try again. I concentrated. As soon as I'd managed to take control briefly three more times, I stopped.

Feeling drained and ready to take it easy, I thanked Emily and waded to shore. When I got to the beach I felt cold, water dripping from my pants. I'd not taken my sandals off as I'd gone in.

Before I could do more than look down at the soggy mess, Emily reached out and placed a hand on the side of my leg. The water quickly left the fabric and fell on the sand.

I watched, thinking the whole experience had been amazing. Whenever I spent time with other elves and saw what they were trying to do, especially combining elements, I was blown away.

And despite being the most powerful in terms of the amount of time I could spend controlling the two elements I'd practiced with, several of the elves could beat me on precision and control.

The Sanctuary had the masters. The last time I'd been there, I'd noticed that the air master tired faster than me. He also didn't have much that I couldn't do as well or better, but the other three masters were still way ahead of my skill level.

Of course, I'd been an air elemental over a year longer than I'd been an earth one, and it was another year later that I was finally getting control of water.

It's tomorrow, Zephyr said. *I'm two tomorrow.*

You say that as if I've forgotten, I replied.

I hadn't, and he knew it. Despite my attempt to arrange a surprise birthday party for him, he'd known about it. He could hear my thoughts, which made hiding something like that impossible.

It was also strange. He was an adult and a mature dragon, yet due to his genetic memories and the wisdom of the past dragons, he was far older in many ways.

Careful. I'm not old, he added a moment later.

I chuckled. There was no way he was old, but I would never deny that it had been a crazy two years. One thing I knew for sure was that Zephyr's memories were invaluable. He knew far more about the elven history of Earth than any books, although there were gaps. He knew very little about the mythicals behind the symbol Erlan had found weeks earlier. Amcika, a cult that wanted the portals open.

It was a worry to both of us that someone in our circle was leaking information about Zephyr and me to an unknown group, but we were none the wiser about why and whether they were a threat.

All Zephyr knew was that the portals had been closed for a good reason, and they wouldn't be easy to open again.

Stop worrying about it, Zephyr said as we wound up the class and I thanked Emily for a third time for helping me learn to control water. *So far, it's simply information, and we've been more careful since.*

I exhaled and felt the waves of comfort Zephyr sent me over our bond. He was right. Until I knew for sure there was a threat, I was keeping myself from enjoying my new life by worrying about it.

And since mythicals were largely trusted and free to go about our lives, I had every intention of enjoying it.

CHAPTER TWO

Despite being free to go where we wanted since the general public had eased off the abuse, it still felt good to return to the warehouse. As we usually did, we landed on the roof and made our way down the ramp into the heart of the building.

It looked different after I'd modified it with my abilities and made the whole building stronger; it was also a lot more stunning now. The walls were rock, and plants grew everywhere as part of the structure and to look beautiful.

Of course, it wasn't as amazing as the Sanctuary, but I'd taken inspiration from the way the earth elementals there had formed the rock from the mountains into buildings, and I was proud of what I'd done to the warehouse.

I felt guilty that the organization had paid to have it modified and made bigger when less than a year later, I'd made a bunch of improvements and proved I could have done everything they'd paid for by myself.

Admittedly, I couldn't have done it when we'd needed

more space to house the mythicals and elves coming to us for refuge, but I still felt bad about it.

If you feel that bad, you could always return the big stack of cash Iris gave us when we were on the run, Zephyr suggested.

I chuckled. We'd agreed to keep it and use it for other mythicals if they needed financial aid of any kind, but I'd not informed Iris of that or done anything but thank her for coming through for us.

Minsheng was one of the first to come to greet us, a look of relief on his face. I hurried to hug him. "I did it," I whispered in his ear. "I can control water."

He pulled back and studied my face for a moment, his mouth hanging open, then broke into a broad grin.

"I knew you would. Gwaelon and Ruehnar are going to be so pleased."

"Yeah. Bialan might not be so excited, though," I replied, mentioning the fire master at the Sanctuary in response to Minsheng talking about the water master and his brother's reactions.

"He'll have hope that fire will follow," Minsheng replied. "We all do."

Emily came running up the stairs a moment later and interrupted us. The rideshare she had taken to the warehouse must have arrived.

"Have you told him?" she asked, looking as if she might burst.

I nodded and laughed at her excitement.

"Yay! Let's celebrate."

I blinked, not sure I wanted a celebration.

"We celebrate when other mythicals gain their ability," Emily said. "You celebrated when I did."

"Aella gained a new element?" Erlan asked as he came up the stairs, carrying his laptop with him.

Once again, I was pressed for information. The news spread through the warehouse, and people in the building came up and congratulated me.

"Okay, we can celebrate," I said eventually. "But nothing big, please."

"All right. I can manage that," Daisy said, grinning at me, then turning toward the kitchen. She grabbed Grim along the way to get him to help her, and the others went to decorate our largest room.

I tried not to worry about that and focused on my Shishou.

"I'm so proud of you," he said a moment later. "But I must call you back to duty. Your liaison with the LAPD has arrived. He's down in the kitchen, waiting to talk about effectively policing mythicals."

Trying not to sigh too loudly, I made my way down the stairs and headed for the kitchen. I knew Daisy and Grim were in there and would probably not want me to have a meeting right under their feet, but it was better than anywhere else in the building.

We didn't usually take meetings, but this would allow the liaison to experience and see part of the life we led in the warehouse. As I reached the kitchen doorway, I stopped. Zephyr almost bumped into me.

At the kitchen table was the police officer who had arrested me several months earlier when the US government decided to charge me for attacking one of their compounds.

The charges had been based on falsified evidence a man

called Jacobs had created to try to keep me from opposing him, but this was the guy who had come to carry out the orders.

He got up when he spotted me and took his cap off.

"It looks like you recognize me, ma'am," he said.

"Please, call me Aella," I replied as I found my ability to move again. I walked up to the table and held my hand out. "And I know you were doing your job the last time we met."

"As were you," he said as he gave me a strong shake. He then focused on Sen and Zephyr, holding his hand out and up. It was a hesitant offer of a handshake, but Sen and Zephyr lowered their heads in a half-nod, half-bow.

Thankfully the cop had enough sense to realize this was their version of the same greeting, and he responded in kind. It was a good start from a mythical liaison, and it made me feel more relaxed.

"Minsheng tells me you're here to discuss how to police our kind," I said, motioning for him to sit down again. There was a mug of coffee in front of him, and Daisy turned and placed another mug in front of me, as well as a bowl of nutrient-rich water for Sen. As Zephyr squeezed into the room and over to one side, she also filled a large bowl of water for him.

The cop in front of me watched as Zephyr drank, putting his mouth down into the bowl. Sen bounded off my shoulder and stuck her feet in hers.

I picked up my mug and cradled it between my hands, finding the warmth radiating from it calming. I ignored everyone as I reached for the liquid with my mind. Slowly I started it turning, pushing it around in circles.

When I looked up, satisfied I had indeed learned to control water, I realized the cop was staring at it.

"Did you stir your drink by looking at it?" he asked.

"Technically, I don't need to look at it, but water is my newest and weakest element, so I looked. I can control air and earth with my eyes closed. I control air automatically now, forming a barrier around myself and making myself move more effortlessly."

The guy's eyes went wide, and his mouth fell open.

"When you were arrested and there was no fuss, I assumed we'd caught you when you were taxed, or you weren't as powerful as everyone made out," he said a moment later. "None of us believed you'd let yourself be taken. Were we wrong? Because if so, I can see no effective way we'll ever be able to police your kind."

"There's no need to panic. You're right that I let you take me, but there are few elves as powerful as I am. For starters, most elves can only control one element. If they do control a second, it's so weak it's negligible."

"Right," he said, "That's something, at least. It seems you've got a lot to tell me about your kind. Shall we start there? Do you mind if I take notes?"

"Take all the notes you need..." I trailed off, hoping he'd offer me his name. I had not gotten it when he'd arrested me, and I couldn't see a badge on him.

"Neil. Please call me Neil."

"Okay, Neil, you take notes while I tell you what I know about mythicals and what we're capable of. Some of the others here can fill in anything I don't know, especially Zephyr. Feel free to interrupt me if you have questions or don't understand something."

The cop nodded and got out paper and pen.

It reminded me of the moment the lawyer who'd defended us had turned up and how he'd sat and listened to us through the early hours of the morning to make sure he could serve us well. It gave me confidence, so I told the man everything I felt was relevant about what we could do and what each type of mythical was like.

While I didn't tell him everything, I did my best to appear trustworthy and give him what he'd need to do his job. I made it clear that the majority of powerful elves answered to the Sanctuary and their council, many of whom were teachers and extremely responsible with their abilities.

I also pointed out how being so much stronger myself would enable me to provide assistance for any situations that might arise in LA, and I reiterated a recommendation to work with the organization to have someone like me in every major city who worked with the police forces to keep everyone safe.

Neil pointed out that he didn't have the authority to authorize something like that, but that he saw the need for it. Finally we talked about the agency Agent Crawley was in charge of and how they knew plenty and could help. It appeared to be news to him, but we talked about what they were likely to do and what information they had that Neil might find useful.

When we finished, several hours had passed, and he'd asked me many questions as well as made many notes. Zephyr had also given him a lot of information about other mythical creatures, making it clear that many were like any other wild animal: harmless if left alone and more scared of humans than humans were of them.

When Erlan came down for lunch with Newton on his shoulder, we showed Neil what the fire salamanders were capable of. He made notes on them as well.

Finally, we appeared to be done.

"I've got a lot to process," he said. "And I'm sure I'm going to have more questions, but for now, it looks as if the best option is to give you a police communicator and have you answer, or another elf you nominate and vouch for when you're off-duty. That way, if we have a hostile situation with another mythical, you can act as backup."

"I'm more than happy to do so," I said. "I understand most police forces go through training as well?"

"Yes, they do."

"Then I'm happy to enroll in any classes necessary. I don't need to know how to fire a gun or anything weapons based but if there are certain elements of ethics, laws to be sure of, I'm more than happy to learn whatever is considered necessary to act as an officer in my own right."

Neil paused and gaped again a moment.

"I... I don't know how the folks higher up would feel about having a mythical on the force, but I can put it to them."

"If they say yes, I'll do it, too," Erlan said, still lingering near me.

"And I'll vouch for him," I added to make sure Neil seriously considered the offer.

"All right. I'll get back to you on everything as soon as I can."

I let Neil leave, noticing Daisy and Grim were almost

finished in the kitchen. Several heavenly-smelling dishes were on their way to the dining room area. I tried not to peek so it would be a nice surprise. I had finished the meeting with the liaison feeling anxious. I'd given them a lot of information about mythicals.

They had a lot anyway. Or at least the agency did, Zephyr reminded me. *He's trying to understand what it would take.*

I sighed. Zephyr was right.

As Daisy disappeared with another large bowl and she instructed Grim to bring up more, I noticed that Erlan was still nearby, his eyes fixed on me.

I gave him my attention, pretty sure he had been hanging around to get a moment to talk to me privately. Not sure where everyone else was, I took him down the corridor toward the small dead end, grateful that Chris wasn't there at the moment tinkering on his projects.

The gnome had turned it into a small workshop where he made gadgets for us, including a material that hid our bodies from heat detectors. There was magic involved, but I'd neglected to tell the police about that. Only Zephyr and I had any of it, and I wasn't about to give up a secret that had saved our lives on multiple occasions yet.

"I've been through the data I have," Erlan whispered as soon as we were sure we were alone. "And I've cross-checked it with the people who were in the building and had access to the computer the information was sent from."

"And?" I replied.

"There's one person who can be leaking the info." As Erlan finished speaking, he turned the laptop around to show me the screen.

I could see the list of everyone living at the warehouse and the times they were in or out for the last two weeks. There was one name that had a full match.

Chris.

Chris was working with a secret group of mythicals intent on reopening the portals.

"Are you sure it's him?" I asked although I suspected the answer would be yes. Erlan was nothing if not thorough, and we'd discussed how sure we needed to be before we accused anyone of anything.

"He's the sole possibility unless someone is somehow controlling the computer remotely to make it look like him. But if that were true..." Erlan shook his head as he trailed off. "They'd be so skilled that we'd never prove it was anyone."

"Okay," I whispered back, hearing Grim and Daisy returning to the kitchen. "Find out what you can about the mythicals behind this banned symbol and send it to me. I'll deal with Chris. We're going to keep everything between us until I have a better idea of what it is he's supporting."

"All right, but if the Sanctuary banned it, it can't be good."

"You're probably right, but Chris has saved my life, and more than once. I'm going to talk to him and give him a chance to explain himself, if nothing else."

Erlan realized that was a good idea. He took his laptop and hurried away. For a moment I didn't move, wanting to cry.

Although I'd known someone in the warehouse was leaking information, I'd assumed it was one of the mythicals we'd taken in along the way. Someone we weren't as attached to. Chris was Minsheng's best friend. He'd been there for us from the beginning.

There might be another explanation, Zephyr said, but he sounded sad as well. I knew he didn't buy it, but I appreciated the encouragement.

Are the portals as bad as everyone thinks? I asked a moment later, wanting to be sure. *If they go to the location mythicals are from, surely having more of our kind around is a good thing?*

If the mythical world existed as it used to, there would be many who were lovely or similar to those in the Sanctuary. And there would be other dragons too. But the portals were closed for a reason. An elf went mad, took control of other elves' mythical bonds, and tried to wipe out or enslave every creature and race elves couldn't bond with. Declared that it was his birthright.

And he's on the other side of these portals? I asked.

Possibly. They trapped him as well. It's possible he's still trapped in the prison the other elves constructed for him, but many doubted it would hold him forever. Locking the portals at this end ensured he couldn't return here, however.

But they locked other mythicals on his side?

Some agreed to be guardians of his prison. Others refused to leave the world they'd always called home. Many on Earth have wished they made the same choice in the last few millennia.

I believed Zephyr's words. Humanity hadn't been kind to mythicals.

At least I had the capacity to do something about it now.

CHAPTER THREE

Stuffed, I leaned into Zephyr. The large dragon had also eaten more than enough. It was rare for either of us to feel full. Our metabolisms both worked on overdrive, with elven abilities regularly draining mine and being a dragon almost always making him hungry. I didn't doubt that I was about to use some of the energy I was digesting pretty swiftly as well.

Before I could decide what to do next or work out if our little celebration was over, Minsheng stood up, Jinto beside him.

"As many of you are aware, Aella has been training hard for years to master the elements, and she's made me a very proud Shishou on more than one occasion."

I felt my cheeks flushing as everyone in the room looked at me.

"She's bonded with two phenomenal mythicals, who I am also honored to know. And today she took another step on the path laid before her. Would you like to show everyone what you learned how to do today, Aella?" Minsheng looked at me, and the room went silent.

"Can I say no to this one?" I asked as I got up.

At the same time, Daisy appeared with a couple of large bowls. One was full of water, and the other was empty. I had a feeling I knew what I was going to be asked to do, but moving water against gravity was harder than stirring a drink or pushing against waves.

Not sure how to begin but aware I had everyone's eyes on me, I let Daisy put them down beside each other before I attempted to connect with the water. She pushed them so close they were touching before she backed off and gave me some space.

No pressure, I thought as I reached to control the water.

You've got this, Zephyr replied. *Take it one step at a time and remember how it felt at the beach.*

While he spoke into my head, acting as a coach, I concentrated and connected with the water. It felt strange at first, as if I was both in the bowl and standing on my feet, but eventually I grew used to it, focusing on what I could get it to do and trying to ignore the people in the room.

After taking a deep breath, I moved the water, starting with lifting it and bringing it to the edge of the bowl near the empty one. It wasn't the easiest thing I'd ever tried to do, but it was easier than controlling air had been the first time.

I continued to move the water higher, watching it form a dome, the effect smoother than I'd expected. I could feel the control draining me, my skill so lacking that I was having to use a lot more energy than I would usually expend on something simple.

Deciding to take the chance, I quickly hurled the water over the side of the bowl and flopped it into the empty waiting one. It splashed out, but my friends and the other mythicals in the building cheered loudly and clapped.

I grinned, looking up as I managed to move the last drop of water across. I was tired, but I knew I'd recover, and it was nice to be cheered for doing something.

As Daisy collected the bowl, a hand clapped me on the shoulder. I turned to see Chris.

"Who knew you'd be this awesome when I picked up you, your baby dragon, and Minsheng in Elysian Park two years ago?" Chris asked. "I must admit I had my doubts, but you've blown me away. You're truly Henera."

I had no idea what he meant by the word Henera, but it was vaguely familiar. Had someone else said it before?

Yes. One of the elves we rescued with Jinto and Ascan called you Henera, Zephyr told me, nuzzling his head against my other side. He'd clearly picked up the wave of emotions I felt—not just about the word, but also about the person using it.

It was strange to talk to Chris after what Erlan had told me.

Before I could say anything else to him, however, Emily came up.

"That was awesome," she said. "It took me ages to be that good at controlling water. You're a natural."

"I think it gets easier after the previous elements," I replied, telling her how long it had taken me to control air and how many bowls I'd broken from one of Minsheng's restaurants.

By the time I had finished telling her about my first lessons, I had her and Zephyr chuckling, and things felt normal again.

Whatever was happening with Chris, I couldn't let it affect every waking moment in the warehouse. Somehow I was going to have to get past it and work out how to broach the subject with him.

It took me another half an hour to finish satisfying everyone's curiosity and telling stories of what I could do. Minsheng was the only person left, other than Zephyr and Sen. He looked at the three of us.

"I can't put into words how grateful and honored I am to Shishou you three," he said, taking my hand and looking at Sen and Zephyr in turn. "Let's get to training and see what interesting things we can do with three elements at once."

I groaned at the mention of training, knowing I was about to be put through more grueling tasks. Part of me wanted to not train as much these days, and we'd lowered the amount of time so I could train others. It still used my abilities in many ways to teach.

Another part of me knew, however, that we'd survived as long as we had because we'd trained regularly and hard. That part of me knew it could never stop. It was the same part of me that worried it wouldn't be long before my powers were needed again. If there were mythicals out there who thought the portals should be opened again, I might be challenged by another force.

I shuddered as I thought about it and followed

Minsheng down the steps into the dojo. Over the years, this room had changed the least. The majority was dedicated to teaching martial arts, archery, and shooting. The rest was mine to use however I needed.

Lyra was in the training section, getting ready for the first lesson of the day. She brought in the majority of the money from non-organization sources, the archery range Ronan had started and the shooting range Daisy managed bringing in the rest. Finally, the mythicals who had jobs outside and could pay rent did so.

Everyone else and the other bills we had were supported by the organization.

Minsheng had income that wasn't tied to the building and the mysterious benefactors who sent us money. He also owned several restaurants in the city, one of them where I'd found him two years earlier.

It seemed as if a lifetime had passed since he'd invited me in and fed Zephyr and me. He'd been the first to recognize me for what I'd become, and despite me running shortly after our first meeting, he'd been there when I'd returned and ever since.

If Minsheng was proud of me, I was equally grateful for him.

Putting thoughts of the old days from my mind, I tried to focus on the here and now. The knowledge of the portals and the events of the day so far made me more anxious to train. I needed to be ready for whatever was in my future. *We* needed to be ready.

Zephyr, Sen, and I moved toward the small desk, where Minsheng had a book open. It wasn't one I recognized, but it was hefty, and Minsheng had clearly been consulting it.

"So, where do you want me to begin today?" I asked.

"I think you've probably taxed the water side of things after the display upstairs. Daisy went to town with those big bowls, so let's practice some simpler stuff with the other two elements to warm up. Then we can think of a way to combine the three."

I wasn't sure how he'd do that, but I liked the idea of trying to do something I knew I was fairly good at. There was something to be said for starting easy. I also liked the idea of having things I could include the others in. I didn't ever want Zephyr and Sen to feel left out or as if they weren't useful. It had happened many times in the past, and it wasn't fair to them.

While we practiced, Minsheng returned to reading his book.

Zephyr, Sen, and I flew around the interior, taking out targets and pushing ourselves to move faster and with more accuracy. I used my abilities to help, and by the time we were done, Zephyr was in human form and stood beside me.

I'd like to try controlling water too, he explained as I raised my eyebrows.

When we had no threats, he rarely took human form except to sleep sometimes. Most of the time, I associated the human form with the romantic element of our bond. While he was a dragon, he was my bonded mythical. That was still intimate, but in a very different way.

Okay, we've probably got minutes before students arrive to train, I reminded him, making sure he knew that we would need him to take dragon form again as soon as the first person checked in for their lesson.

He gave me a nod and stepped closer to our Shishou.

There was a glass of water on the shelf behind Minsheng. The part-dwarf glanced at it and then at Zephyr, who was so focused on the water in the container that he was unaware he'd been noticed.

It took a couple of minutes, but eventually, the water started turning. In much the same way that I'd stirred my coffee earlier, Zephyr was controlling the drink Minsheng or someone else had abandoned earlier in the day.

It continued to get faster, the edges rising as the center dipped and swirled, causing a vortex. I was about to suggest Zephyr stop. Something about the setup felt wrong.

A moment later, there was a loud bang as the glass shattered.

I grabbed it and the air around it and did my best to direct it to the floor or away from people and belongings.

A few slivers of glass came through my control and embedded in the wooden desk Minsheng was sitting at, and more hit his chair.

I managed to get the rest to the floor, and Zephyr looked worried. "Oops. I think I found the resonant frequency of the glass."

Minsheng looked at the tiny shards that could have cut him open and the mess on the floor, and I thought he was going to lose his temper. Instead, he glanced my way.

"Well, that's a new one. Pretty effective form of attack," Minsheng said, apparently not bothered by narrowly missing being cut to ribbons.

Before either Zephyr or I could do it again to work out how it had happened and try to stop it happening unless we needed it, I heard the sound of the first students arriving in the changing rooms above.

Zephyr let out a small sigh at having to change into his dragon body and walked into a larger space. A moment later, he morphed into the tall, strong dragon he was.

It still took me by surprise to see him change and how swift it was. Before another few seconds had passed, I had Zephyr in dragon form leaning his head against mine.

His smooth scales were warm, and they made me feel relaxed. Everything was right when I was with Sen and Zephyr. The myconid seemed to appreciate the dragon form of Zephyr since she jumped from my shoulder onto the top of his head and scurried down his back. She found a perch and sat.

"What are you reading about?" I asked Minsheng when I noticed he'd returned to his book.

"Water elementals. I confess it's the element I know the least about. Because I strongly suspected any elemental elf I found in LA would be fire- or air-based, I didn't study this one as much as I probably ought to have."

I smiled, knowing Minsheng's idea of not studying something very much was far more rigorous than someone else's idea of studying a lot.

"Jinto has lent me a book," my Shishou continued. "It has some interesting differences. And there's a great list of possible mythicals to bond with. I don't know if we'd find many in LA, but it's probably worth looking for some."

Minsheng kept talking, but I zoned out, caught by a thought. Another mythical to bond with. I'd been aware that was a possibility, but I knew things had changed when

I'd bonded with Sen. It had also been touch and go if Sen would come with me.

To bond with another new creature wasn't a small thing to consider. It was another being to share my thoughts and feelings with. Another creature that would leak their feelings into me.

There were a lot of up sides and down sides to something like bonding, and I wasn't sure I was ready for something like that right now.

If you don't like the creature you're bonded with, it is possible to break a bond, Zephyr said. *Most elves don't because the odds of finding another creature to bond with these days are slim. Especially of certain types of mythical.*

I exhaled, grateful once again for Zephyr as he sent me reassuring waves, but I felt guilty. I loved Sen and Zephyr in different ways. I was bonded with them, and I couldn't bear the idea of not having them in my world.

Sen like bond, the wood dryad said, and I scooped her up and gave her a gentle cuddle. The movement let Minsheng know I'd stopped paying attention.

"Where did you switch off?" he asked, not bothering to get irritated. I had a feeling he was resigned to my mind wandering and my bonded conversations distracting me from the world outside our bubble.

"When you mentioned me looking for another bond. I don't know how we feel about introducing a fourth creature."

"No, of course not. Forgive me. I will never bond the way you have. I had momentarily forgotten that it can be an intense period and cause many emotions and tensions.

It must be worse when you have more than one. We'll do what we can at your pace."

I smiled as Minsheng hugged me, grateful for him and everything else I had.

As we finished up our training, however, I couldn't help but think of Chris again. The gnome might be betraying us, and it was going to tear Minsheng apart if it was true. How on earth was I going to tell him?

CHAPTER FOUR

"Aella," Chris said. I froze as I walked toward the roof.

"I was going out," I said. "Zephyr wants to stretch his wings, and the beach is wonderful at this time of evening."

I felt guilty. I was supposed to be working out if Chris was betraying us, and here I was avoiding him. I felt waves of comfort wash over me, coming from Zephyr, who'd stopped farther up with Sen on his back.

"Mind if I join you? I've got prototypes of some more gadgets for you, Sen, and Zephyr to test," he said.

My mouth fell open, and for a moment, I couldn't speak.

It's a good opportunity, Zephyr said. *You can talk to him away from everyone else and while we're somewhere we know well and are relatively safe.*

I knew Zephyr was right, so I shrugged and tried to look normal.

"Sure. New gadgets sound fun," I replied. "Meet us there?"

Chris nodded, put his thumbs up, and hurried down the

stairs toward his little workshop. Trying to ignore the knot in my stomach, I caught up with Zephyr.

While he was right that it was a good opportunity, I wasn't sure I wanted to take it yet. Trying not to panic or worry, I focused on the air around me and powering up off the roof.

Zephyr followed me a moment later, flying up until I could land on his back and use the air to help us both fly. We made our way straight to the beach with the sun low in the sky and beginning to set.

This was one of my favorite times of day, and for a moment I felt free, chasing the sun with Zephyr.

Although there was no way we could catch it, I loved flying toward it, the ocean reflecting the glowing orb at us. It was a very calm day, and the ocean was like a millpond in places, still, glittering, and sparkling. I spotted fish, a dolphin pod, and several boats.

The beach was still relatively busy; others were also there to see the sunset. Turning, Zephyr flew along the length of it, and I waved at people we passed by. Not everyone was paying attention, but some shouted our names, and many waved.

It was fun greeting so many people, and it made me wonder how different my life might have been if I'd been one of the people on the ground instead of in the air.

Although I loved loads of things about my current life, including everyone in it, a small part of me longed for something simpler. Something where I was an average Joe going about a normal life, with a normal job, a house, and maybe a partner. Someone steady and reliable who didn't care if we had kids.

I'm steady and reliable, and I don't care if we have kids, Zephyr said, amused.

True, I replied. *You do have those qualities. And in general, also being a dragon is a pretty big plus.*

Talking about kids did make me wonder, though. Would they be dragons, elves, or something else?

They would be elves, Zephyr replied. *Or they could choose to be human. I would need to be in human form, so our elven natures would dominate the genetics, and they would be able to choose. As you have done, if subconsciously.*

I sighed, feeling the deep sadness in him. It might mean the end of his kind.

My kind was doomed with me. It's why I don't mind if we have children or not.

Before I could think of anything else, I felt waves of compassion and warmth come from Sen, along with a hint of her sadness.

Sen alone before. But not now. Has bond.

It was the longest set of words the small myconid had ever uttered, and it made me sadder. What if their kinds existed on the other side of the portals? Was it worth the risk of trying to open them?

No, Zephyr's voice boomed. *As much as I'd love for there to be more dragons, it can't happen. Not ever. It's not worth the risk. We weren't ever supposed to be on this world anyway.*

As Zephyr spoke, he banked and brought us down to the beach. Chris would be waiting for us, and I had a feeling there would be no arguing with Zephyr on this one. And given he had memories from before the portals were closed, I had no intention of trying to sway him.

We found Chris standing beside a large van, looking at

the beach and the sea on a quiet stretch to the south of our usual spot. I wasn't sure it would be quiet for long, but we landed, and I wandered over to the gnome.

He quickly opened the van and pulled out something small and mechanical. It appeared to have straps and a container.

"This is for Sen," he said. "It's a jet pack. It should help her fly, and it comes with a little hat she can wear to make herself float or glide. Essentially means she would land fine if you ever dropped her while flying."

My eyes went wide as I looked at the piece of gear Chris was handing me. He'd made something like this especially for Sen, but he was betraying us. It made no sense. Had there been a mistake?

I tried to put the thoughts behind me as I clipped the prototype on Sen. She grinned up at me as she took the controls, and Chris explained to her what it did.

"This should work fine, but on the off chance it doesn't, be ready to catch her, please," Chris cautioned.

For a moment, I was worried. Was this a trap?

I don't think so, Zephyr said. *He appears to be telling the truth, and he's showing no signs of deception.*

That's something, at least.

We'll work out what's going on, don't worry. For now, though, let Sen play. If we have something for her to fly with, great.

It made sense and helped calm me. As soon as I was fine, Sen climbed onto my shoulder, and I walked farther out on the sand. It would be a softer landing if things went wrong.

Before I could worry or react in any way, Sen jumped

into the air and pressed the controls to ignite the little jet pack. She shot forward several feet, so light she powered through the air.

Sen fly, she declared as she eased off. The extra material attached to the mushroom top and along her back rippled out and acted as wings. Soaring along, she circled us like a miniature version of a glider.

I'd never seen her beam with such delight, and I found myself smiling. It was awesome to see her flying the same way Zephyr and I could, even if she was using technology to do it.

"That works better than I hoped it would," Chris exclaimed, clapping his hands and turning to the van.

I was pretty sure he hadn't brought such a large van with him so he could give Sen something so small, and the next thing I knew, he was lowering a ramp and pulling out what looked like a small boat. After that, he pulled out flippers and another contraption.

"Here," he said, handing me the flippers.

"You want me to swim?

"For a bit. It's more that it will be easier if you're in the water. I confess, this prototype isn't for you. I promised to help with some environmental stuff. It's a combination of magic and technology, but it needs a water elf to start it running, so I figured I'd kill two birds with one stone."

I lifted my eyebrows as he loaded his box-like contraption onto the boat and started dragging it toward the water.

A moment later, I lifted it with my powers and floated it down there instead.

"Oh, I forgot you could do that," he said, grinning at me.

It was hard to know how to respond, so I looked away and out to sea. Sen flew after us, still gliding above my head. Now and then she'd catch a draft, and it would lift her again. If she sank too low, she tucked her legs and turned the little jet pack on until she was higher.

"How much is left in that tank?" I asked Chris, concerned that she was wasting the fuel and it wouldn't be easy to replace.

"Oh, plenty. She just needs a tiny amount, and I can fill a thousand of those little bottles with what we have. She might as well practice while it's safe to do so."

I exhaled with relief, and Sen let out a delighted whoop. It made sense for her to get as good at it as she could, but she was a natural. That might be because she bounded about like a spinning top anyway, but possibly because she was flying the way I did.

Not long after that, I put the boat down at the edge of the water, and Chris checked the engine, the oars, and everything else he needed.

"Right, I've got to get this out to sea, then I need to get it in the water and get the water flowing through it. I could do with your help with the last. Once it's started, it will keep going by itself." Chris then pushed the majority of the boat into the water.

You should get in the boat with him, Zephyr said.

I was lingering on the shore, but I knew Zephyr was right. I just needed to ask Chris. This was my opportunity to find out what was going on.

Acting as if I'd intended to get in the whole time, I pushed the boat out for Chris and flew over and into it so I wouldn't get wet yet. At the same time, Zephyr launched into the air, and he and Sen flew after us, circling around if they got too far ahead.

Chris took the tiller and started the boat's little motor to move us farther out to sea.

"We need to get far enough out the tide won't sweep this thing straight to shore. It can move around and it has GPS and other cool gizmos built in, but it's not hugely powerful."

I nodded as if I understood what we were doing. I was in a boat with Chris, and I wasn't sure what to say or do. How did I ask him if he was a traitor?

"I must admit, it's strange having everyone like us again," Chris said as a couple on another boat waved at us and pointed up excitedly at Zephyr and Sen.

"You're telling me. I'm glad we can come out during the day," I replied, motioning at the sunset. It was almost done, but out on the water, it was more spectacular.

"You know there's a lot of mythicals very grateful for what you've done. You've made this world safe for us again. After so many millennia."

"Not necessarily the whole world. But more of it for sure."

"It's a huge win and huge progress. Makes me wonder what it could be like if there were more mythicals. Do you ever wonder?"

"Not sure what you mean?" I replied, thinking Chris might be leading me onto the subject.

"If mythicals were as numerous as it talks about in the books when Tuviel and Azargad were alive. There's more of them out there somewhere. On another planet or in another dimension."

"Through the portals?" I glanced at Chris, trying to look as if it was a normal gesture.

He was staring at me as he steered us out.

"Yeah. I think so," he said. "They closed those, though."

"I understand that was for a good reason," I replied, trying to make it sound like a throwaway comment. I couldn't quite believe this conversation was happening. It was as if he was fishing for my reaction and thoughts on the matter.

"Apparently. It's pretty extreme, shutting us off from our kind here, but they didn't think we were safe. Of course, with you around, we're safer than we've ever been."

"You sure about that?" I asked. "We barely managed to beat Jacobs."

"True, but you're more powerful now than you were then, and you've gained another element. By the time you have the four mastered, you're going to rival Kirdash himself."

In my head, Zephyr growled. I didn't understand an anger washing over me.

"Kirdash?" I asked, feeling Zephyr flinch as I did.

"Yeah, the elf they said went mad and tried to take the bonded mythicals for an extra-powerful army of his own."

Instantly I understood. Zephyr had memories of his ancestors being forced into a bond with the elf. I frowned and looked at the beach. We'd come a long way out, but I still didn't have anything definite.

"This is probably far enough," Chris replied as he followed my gaze and took in the distance.

For a moment, our conversation was focused solely on getting his contraption into the water. He showed me where the water needed to flow in and how it would power a motor that would then keep it turning and keep pulling in more water.

Although I had some questions, I cared less about the device than the conversation we'd been having. As soon as the floating cube was in the water, I reached in as well and connected with the water near it.

Chris held out the flippers, but I shook my head and concentrated. If I got it running before it got too far away, I was pretty sure I wasn't going to need to put them on and dive in.

A moment later, I managed to control and push enough water through that I could feel it whirring up and beginning to spin and suck in water of its own accord. While I was doing it, I was pretty sure it had begun pulling in water itself, however, making me wonder if my input had been unnecessary. If it was, I didn't plan on pointing out that I'd noticed. Not yet.

To be sure, however, I stopped the water again and waited, feeling the water particles move without my guidance, and slowly but surely it started back up, each small movement of water that pushed through giving it more energy to ramp up.

"There. Done it, I think. Got it wrong at first, but it's sucking in water now," I said, focusing on it so Chris wouldn't hear me lie.

"Brilliant. Let's head to shore."

I nodded. It was time to find out once and for all what Chris was up to.

CHAPTER FIVE

Taking a couple of deep breaths, I tried to think about the best way to introduce the subject of the portals again.

"I can't believe you need these," Chris said. "You're growing so fast, Aella. It makes me so proud to know you and to have been there at the beginning. When I joined the organization, I had no idea how much I'd gain by being part of their most major prophecy."

"Yeah, well, life takes us in strange directions sometimes. And people seem pretty happy to think I'm going to be amazing. I suppose at least I've gotten the saving everyone part out of the way. Mythicals are safe once more."

"Maybe. But I'd be wary of thinking your job is done," he replied. "Things have a way of surprising us, and there are more mythicals out there. The other side of those portals. You're their savior, too."

I paused and looked at Chris, trying to read his expression.

He's twisting things, Zephyr said a moment later. *Trying to make it sound as if the portals being opened is part of your destiny. It's not. It would invite Him here.*

I decided enough was enough.

"I know what you've been doing," I said to steer the conversation. "I know you've been telling another group of mythicals about what I'm capable of. I know this was more of a test than a need. I know you want those portals open. What I don't understand is why you'd betray Minsheng like this. He has trusted you far longer than I've known you."

As I spoke I grew angrier. I spat the last few words.

Chris' eyes narrowed and he tensed his jaw before responding.

"All I've done has been to aid the organization. You are Henera, the elf who's supposed to save us all. But to do that, the portals need to be opened, and you must go through them to face Kirdash."

Again Zephyr growled.

What's the problem with his name? I asked Zephyr.

It was believed that speaking it could give him power and allow him to home in on the words spoken around it.

Even on another planet? I asked.

Who knows? I don't intend to tempt it.

Noted.

I thought for a moment before looking at Chris again. The boat was almost at the shore, but I was pretty sure our conversation was going to be done before we were on solid ground.

"You might think you're helping me or our kind, but opening a portal to an unknown place where you know evil is waiting is foolish at best and suicidal at worst. The mythicals don't want it open, and the memories of what happened last time are enough for me to know it's a very bad idea."

Chris opened his mouth to speak again, leaning forward. Not sure what else to do to keep him silent, I pushed him into his seat with air and blasted the very words out of his mouth and away from me. He gaped.

"Now, you've got two options. Drop this right here and come to the warehouse with me. We'll make no more mention of this, ever. Spare Minsheng any pain, and you will do what you should have done a long time ago and sever any connection with any mythicals or groups that want the portals open. No more information on me will pass to anyone by your hands ever again."

"Or?"

"Or you can come to the warehouse. You'll have an hour to pack up your belongings and never come back. You can explain your actions to Minsheng if you wish, or I will once you're gone."

"And that's it," Chris snapped back, clearly angry.

"That's it. I won't open those portals, and I won't encourage anyone else to. None of the mythicals here deserve having me play God with their lives. I will never change my mind."

Chris glared at me, but I merely stared back, waiting to see how he reacted.

"You're making a huge mistake. Those portals need to be opened. There are mythicals on the other side who—"

Once again, I cut him off.

"No. There might be mythicals on the other side. Or

Him. I can't take that risk, and you shouldn't ask me to. This conversation is over."

So Chris couldn't argue any further with me. I flew up and out of the boat, rocking it before I used my abilities to lift it out of the water. I floated it to the van and put it inside, Chris still sitting by the tiller.

He had the sense to turn the engine off, and he hurried out of the van as I reconvened with Zephyr and landed on the dragon's back.

"Two choices," I called down to Chris. "I'm going to the warehouse now. When you know what you want to do, return as well."

Zephyr wheeled to one side as Sen landed on me. Stopping her little jetpack and pulling the hat off, she returned to looking like a normal myconid. Her mouth was downturned at the edges, and I sighed as I realized I felt similarly.

This had been a difficult day and had gone from high to low incredibly swiftly. I tried not to let it get to me and instead focused on being where I loved to be, flying with Zephyr and Sen.

You did the right thing, Zephyr said a moment later. *He has no idea what he's talking about. It would mean death for many people on this planet. He used to wipe out anyone he thought was inferior. Every human would be murdered or enslaved. It—*

I know. It's okay. We won't let it happen. No one is going to open those portals. We'll make sure of it.

It's a good thing they can't be opened easily, he replied a moment later.

How hard is it?

44

They require the combined effort of several elven elementals, and very skilled ones at that. A different alignment and strength for each portal, but they require at least three elements at once. And my memories contain discussions of other possible obstacles. No single person could have opened one until today.

I exhaled, not sure I could breathe when I heard Zephyr's words. It sounded as if he'd told me I was the only mythical on earth who could open a portal by myself.

Yes, Zephyr said. *I believe that's why Chris is showing his hand now.*

I shuddered as if the cold had gotten to me. Not sure I liked what he was suggesting, I tried to put it out of my mind. It was bad enough that Chris was about to betray us. We could only hope he got some sense and decided to come to the warehouse and stick to helping us and refrain from passing on info.

But had he told this deluded group of mythicals about my third element or not? I had no way of knowing, but Erlan might.

It was yet another complication in the long line of problems and issues I had before me.

We'll find a way through like everything else. Zephyr's voice was soothing and helped me settle my emotions. At the same time, he flew a loop of the city, not heading straight to the warehouse but giving me time to calm down.

Zephyr was right. We'd been through a lot together. This was a small hurdle. It wasn't at the level of the whole world hating us like before. It wasn't an entire government. It was mythicals who had gotten crazy notions about some portals I'd never open for them.

I was still reassuring myself when Zephyr landed on the roof of the warehouse and we made our way inside. As soon as we were under the roof, I took the little suit Chris had made Sen and the hat that went with it.

It was amazingly well made, and it brought my feelings to the surface once more. How could Chris have been betraying us on the one hand while making us such amazing equipment on the other?

After giving my nearest limb a quick hug as if she understood everything I was feeling without me uttering a word, Sen jumped down and scurried deeper into the building, leading the way.

It made me smile and feel better that the tiny myconid was still eager to be in the large building. She'd been a lot happier in it since I'd modified it and grown plants around it like it was a small piece of forest in a lake of concrete and buildings.

Despite her hurry, I plodded into the building, not sure what to do or where to go while Chris made up his mind. I kept finding myself imagining what I'd do if he decided to go.

Lyra was in the dojo and coming to the end of a lesson. People were arriving for the next. They distracted me and I made small talk, chatting about how their lessons were going and if I'd be around to join them sometime soon.

Now I wasn't considered a threat anymore and the truth about Jacobs had been publicly announced, I was a minor celebrity, and the dojo was busier than ever. I waved to Lyra and considered joining them, but Minsheng appeared, coming up the front stairs and clearly searching for me.

He didn't say anything but motioned for me to head his way. A chill ran up my spine, but I went over to him anyway. Zephyr was on that side of the room, having stayed out of the way while people were changing. His large body was almost too big for this room.

Minsheng led us down the stairs and into the kitchen off the entry.

He then shut the door. Daisy, Sen, Ascan, and Holfin were in the room, the latter getting Sen a drink so she could stick her feet in.

They looked at me, and I was pretty sure they realized something was up.

"What happened with Chris?" Minsheng asked as I sat down. "He's returned, and he's started packing up his stuff."

"Gave a bunch of his prototypes to me and told me how to finish them," Daisy said.

"Then he's made his mind up. I promised him I wouldn't say anything without giving him the chance to speak for himself. If he doesn't want to tell you why, I will do so once he's gone."

Minsheng came over to me and turned me to face him.

"What happened?" he demanded again.

"I'm sorry, Minsheng. I had hoped he wouldn't be doing this, and that if he did, he'd tell you himself. I won't say."

"Did you ask him to leave?"

"No, not exactly." I looked at Zephyr, not sure if I was handling this right. I'd never been in this situation.

The large dragon stepped closer, gently nudging Minsheng with his head. The Shishou backed up, his face showing the hurt and confusion he felt.

"Not everything has been as it seemed with Chris for

some time. He has been...wrestling with questions. Aella talked to him this evening, and it became clear that he needed to make a choice. It appears that he has chosen to leave." Zephyr lowered his head. "This is as sad to us as it is you, although perhaps less painful. Please, if you must know why, ask him to explain."

Minsheng looked at us for a moment, then stormed out of the room and rushed toward the corridor where Chris performed his experiments and built his prototypes.

I didn't get up, able to hear as Minsheng confronted Chris.

"What are you doing, Chris?" he asked loud enough everyone could hear.

"Leaving. I have work to do, and it's clear I can't do it here any longer."

"But why?"

"Go ask your precious ward. I've offended her sensibilities, and she's made it clear she can't embrace the future she's created. If you manage to talk some sense into her, I'll consider coming back."

I frowned, not sure what to say to that kind of accusation. I wanted to defend myself, angry that he was trying to put the blame on me, but I'd done what I thought was best. There was no way I would be used to open portals when I didn't agree with it. It wouldn't matter what any of them said.

He also betrayed us, Zephyr pointed out, moving closer to me and resting his head on my lap.

Sen also came closer, leaving little wet footprints on the table as she hopped out of her drink to cuddle against my neck.

"Right. I'm going to start getting dinner on," Daisy said. "Maybe by the time we've finished eating, we'll know what the hell is going on. In the meantime, it will give me something to do."

Ascan moved to the door and closed it before giving me an apologetic look, but I appreciated it. Waiting for Minsheng to return and listening to Chris say spiteful things wasn't something I wanted to do.

Without encouragement, I got to my feet and helped Daisy chop vegetables. It would keep my hands busy while I waited for my Shishou to return and for Chris to leave.

CHAPTER SIX

Dinner was almost ready by the time Minsheng returned. Erlan came with him. The young elf had his laptop and a worried look on his face. I tried not to be concerned, but I gave them my attention.

"He's gone," Minsheng said, sounding tired.

"Did he explain?" I asked, not expecting him to have said anything I'd agree with.

"Not exactly, but Erlan heard enough he came to set things straight. There was proof Chris has been working for Amcika all this time," Minsheng said.

Daisy dropped the saucepan she was holding, the food and water it contained sloshing over the side and hissing on the hot stove.

Holfin rushed to help her clean up and make sure she wasn't hurt. I used my powers to move the water into the pan and blow the steam away from her, which got me a nod of gratitude.

"What's Amcika?" I asked.

"That symbol I showed you," Erlan said. "Minsheng says it's the name of the group behind it."

It was clear that was new to Erlan since he glanced at Minsheng to check if he'd said it right. Our Shishou nodded.

"He asked me to consider opening the portals. I said no, then I asked him why he'd been giving this group info on me," I explained.

"After giving me a crappy response about how I was dooming every mythical on the other side of the portals and not stepping into my destiny, I told him he either needed to drop connections with this group or leave. He's chosen to leave."

Daisy put everything down again and came over and hugged me.

"You did the right thing. Those portals shouldn't be opened. And Amcika is thought badly of for a good reason," Daisy said, but I noticed the look of fear she gave Minsheng.

"What is it?" I asked. "What are you not telling me?"

"The dreams we had that led us to the organization. They were of armies that came through the portals. Armies of mythicals who believed what Tuviel's greatest foe did."

"Yes, Chris said his name as if it was nothing. Zephyr assures me I shouldn't repeat it."

"The thing is, the only way it's possible for that battle to happen is if the portals are reopened. Maybe not all of them, but most of them." Daisy shuddered.

"I won't open them," I said again.

"That might be enough." Minsheng exhaled, then looked at us.

I could see him trying to hide the hurt he clearly felt, but he didn't look at me again.

"We should eat, and then we'll decide what to do. The Sanctuary should be warned. Chris has been there many times, and we don't know what he told Amcika about the place. And I should talk to the organization. They've been duped, and they'll want to heighten security at the portal sites they protect."

I blinked, as shocked by Minsheng's latest admission as I was about everything else I'd learned that day.

Worn out by the eventful day, however, I eagerly tucked into the meal despite how subdued it was. Sen returned to her drink, and Zephyr chowed down on as much food as I'd ever seen him eat.

As soon as we'd finished, I felt tired, but I couldn't rest. If anyone was going to the Sanctuary to warn them, it had to be Zephyr, Sen, and me.

Fly? Sen asked, getting up and grinning at Zephyr and me.

I couldn't help but smile at her desire to get into the air. It was one of the best things about our bond. Having the three of us in the air was heaven.

Minsheng picked up on the movement and got to his feet as well.

"Stay there as long as you need. And try not to worry," he said as he went to the cupboard and grabbed snacks.

Daisy got us drink bottles and held them out. I looked at the pair, grateful for the care and understanding they were showing.

"Want to come?" I asked Erlan. The elf was still sitting at the table, focused on his laptop screen.

"No." He shook his head. "I want to see if I can find out what Chris told Amcika and if there's anything we can find out about them. Where they are, how many of them, etc."

I nodded and sighed, glad someone else was thinking about that element.

"We'll handle the organization. If anything comes up, we'll message you," Minsheng said.

Not convinced he was okay without me there after having Chris betray him, I gave him a hug.

"I'm sorry," I whispered as I did. "I know he's been a friend for a long time."

Minsheng didn't reply, but he gave me a tighter squeeze before letting go.

Let's fly, Zephyr said. *I could do with the cool night and some fresh air.*

You and me both, I replied as I reached for Sen. She bounded onto my shoulder, then slipped into the front of my jacket. It felt familiar having her there in the position one she often adopted while we were flying.

I relaxed as soon as we were in the air and tried to forget my worries. While Chris had let us down, and it hurt in a way I still couldn't describe, I felt a certain amount of relief from having everyone else at the warehouse agree with how we'd handled the situation and our desire not to open the portals.

Everything Daisy and Minsheng had said added extra worry, however. They'd mentioned the dreams that had taken them to the organization before, but I'd assumed they were dreams of Tuviel and Azargad. Or not something I truly needed to worry about. They were mentioned in passing as if they had done everything they were supposed to.

That's still possible, Zephyr said. We were flying just over the tops of the buildings in LA, heading east toward the mountains and the Sanctuary.

I know, but I think Daisy and Minsheng are worried it's a prophetic vision.

Yes. I got that impression as well.

The serious tone to Zephyr's reply made me more concerned. Could the portals be opened without us? I had no idea, but I knew I wasn't going to open any. No matter what happened, I would refuse.

Be careful what you say never to, Zephyr replied. *We can never be certain, just aware of our current intentions. If we knew it was safe on the other side, it would be amazing to open them.*

No one seems to think it's safe, I said as I considered the possibility. More of my kind *would* be amazing, even if it ran the risk of upsetting the balance we'd recently found with humanity.

They don't. And they're right, but that doesn't change that it's possible.

I sighed, wondering why everything had to be so complicated.

We flew the rest of the way in silence, the stars and moon out above us. As we went over the forest I'd found Sen in, I felt the small myconid shift in my jacket as if she were trying to look down and see it.

Sen, want to land? I asked.

Sen fine, she replied a moment later. *Sen check trees safe.*

I reached out with my mind, feeling for the plants down

there. I hoped she could also feel the connection. That seemed to satisfy her. She snuggled against me and relaxed.

Once again, it reminded me that there could be another of us soon, which might change the dynamic between us yet again. I still wasn't sure I wanted to think about it, but equally, I wanted to be open to a future that made me stronger and more resilient.

The Sanctuary came into view before I could decide one way or the other. Zephyr and Sen both reassured me they wouldn't mind if I bonded with another creature. They pointed out how it would grow our family, a family neither had had before we'd bonded.

It made it clearer that I hadn't either. An orphan who hadn't gotten along very well with her adoptive parents.

I had a better relationship with them now that I wasn't on the government's most-wanted list, but they lived in another state, and I didn't pay them many visits. I confused them when they tried to be supportive.

I landed near the border, choosing once again to walk over the boundary line and respect the Sanctuary's process for admitting arrivals. As soon as I landed, I saw a track forming in the dirt that led toward the road. A possible reason was deeper in the trees.

A large Jeep stood at the end of the track, barely inside Sanctuary borders. The usual border guard was watching from a small tower nearby. I waved, and the greeting was returned.

As Sen bounded to the ground and I slid off Zephyr's back for the three of us to walk in together, I noticed some of the council coming this way with my lawyer and a couple of humans I didn't recognize. One carried a briefcase, and Robert was talking to Sierrathen about something.

We moved closer, but I was wary of interrupting. Robert and Sierrathen spotted me at the same time, and the lawyer I'd needed when Jacobs was hounding me waved me over.

Sierrathen smiled too, and she gave me a soft bow in the manner the centaurs of the Sanctuary did. I felt acknowledged enough to approach them.

"And talking of how wonderful it is to have mythicals and humans working together on something," Robert said as I came into speaking distance, "meet Aella, Zephyr, and Sen. They are the three mythicals responsible for bringing the recent conflict to an end."

"We didn't do it alone," I replied, embarrassed. Thankfully the man and woman with Robert didn't seem to mind, and they held out their hands to shake mine.

I quickly reintroduced Sen and Zephyr, making it clear they were sentient creatures and part of any conversation I was in.

For a moment, Zephyr talked to the woman about being one of the most majestic creatures on earth and able to fly. The guy told Sen he had a mushroom collection and had several that looked like miniature versions of her. He said it was fascinating to see one with such humanoid characteristics.

Sen took this latter point as it was meant—a conversation starter and an attempt to relate to her.

"Sen dryad," she replied. "Myconid."

"I'm very pleased to make your acquaintance. I hope it's

not rude of me to ask, but could I take a photo?" The man looked at me and Zephyr and Sen.

I took a moment to process the request, but it wasn't the first time people had wanted to pose with the group, so I nodded. The two unknown humans stood with me, Zephyr, and Sen while Robert took a photo with each of their cell phones and another with his.

All the while, Sierrathen and Ronan watched, bemused looks on their faces.

As we relaxed again, I showed Sierrathen one of the images on the phone and told her the humans would be able to show anyone else as well.

"Oh. A proof or way of recording a memory," she replied. "Yes. I believe Lorcan occasionally used a similar device to capture these."

I tried not to smile at her naivety when others in the Sanctuary were quicker to embrace human technology, but it wasn't easy. Thankfully Robert rescued me, coughing and holding up the briefcase he carried.

When I raised my eyebrows, he grinned.

"Contract signed. The land officially belongs to the Sanctuary and is to be governed by the council elected from the mythicals present," he explained a moment later.

I blinked in shock, in awe and excited for the Sanctuary and everyone in it. The President had promised me he'd make it happen, and it appeared as if no one had wasted time.

"This is a huge cause for celebration," Sierrathen said, "And something that wouldn't have been possible without your aid, Aella, Zephyr, and Sen. You arrive at a good time to join the celebrations and be honored for your part in bringing the Sanctuary to what will hopefully be its final home."

I nodded, trying to smile, but if Sierrathen or Ronan picked up on my reluctance, neither of them said anything in front of the humans. Instead, they were ushered to the waiting vehicle, and we waited for them to leave.

Only then did the two council members turn to us with less than jubilant looks.

"It is rare these days that you fly to us so late at night without good reason," Sierrathen said a moment later. "Does something worry you?"

"I do have bad news, I'm afraid. We've discovered that one of our friends, one of the mythicals living in the warehouse, has been working with a group called Amcika."

Both council members gasped, and I felt awful about having to break the news.

"I'm afraid it gets worse. They came here with me on more than one occasion."

Sierrathen sighed and nodded.

"Come. We should talk to the council and tell them everything. They will want to know what danger this might pose."

"I hope none to you," I said. "I believe they've been waiting for me to be able to control three elements to persuade me to open the portals once more."

Sierrathen glanced my way as we strode toward the mountains and the buildings the elves had constructed out of the rocks and plants. I was late enough that some mythicals had retired to sleep, but others were still up, and many waved to me as I passed them by.

Doing my best to appear cheerful and alarm no one

when they had achieved a great moment for their city, I waved and smiled.

Even when we had time to ourselves, Sierrathen didn't ask what I had meant by my last remark, and I gave no indication I intended to explain. It needed to wait until we were before the council.

CHAPTER SEVEN

By the time we reached the council chambers, the whole group was there. Vestan came over to take Sierrathen's hand with a large smile that lit up his eyes.

Everyone hurried over smiling equally broadly, and Martyl, a fairy who had never been particularly warm toward me, fluttered his wings and landed in front of me. He gave me a solemn bow, and I returned the gesture.

"Thank you for your part in this. You've faced a lot to make the mythicals safer, and you have my gratitude."

"I'd do the same again," I replied. "I'm one of your kind no matter where I was born."

"My apologies for doubting your heart. Even if I disagreed with your methods, I should have seen how true it was."

"Apology accepted. And please, forgive me if I wasn't always as understanding as I should have been. I still have a lot to learn about the mythical races, but I'm doing my best to rectify that."

"Come visit me in my little den sometime, and I'll tell

you more of the fairies. My wife would like you, and the kids adore Sen."

I bowed again, surprised by the confession Martyl had made. He had a family, and they knew about us.

As I bowed, I caught Sen's eye. The myconid's head was tilted up so she could grin at me.

Sen like fairies. Fairies full of mischief but care for forest.

Fairies sound amazing, I replied.

"Forgive us," Sierrathen said a moment later, lifting her voice above the din. Elowan and Hargraed had been thanking Zephyr and discussing something else.

Everyone looked at the slender elf in her long, flowing clothes and waited for her to continue speaking.

"While I'm sure you wish to begin celebrating our most recent success, and I think many plans should be made to do so tomorrow for the whole city, Aella brings news of concern. I believe we should hear her words and offer her our wisdom."

I tried not to react to the arrogance in her words and instead respect them for the way in which they were probably meant. I bowed again, looking at Ronan as my focal point.

Of all the council members, he was the one I felt most connected to. I'd fought beside him many times, and we'd mourned the loss of his predecessor Lorcan together. The centaur had died to save my life.

Ronan had also been my security at the warehouse before his commitment to the Sanctuary. Lorcan's death had put him on the council.

Although the councilors glanced at each other, as much in shock as they were curious, they hurried to their seats. I stood before them, Zephyr at my side and Sen on my shoulder.

I paused for a moment, trying to decide what to say as tears welled up. They had been celebrating, and so had I before this came to light. Celebrating the new power I had and the element I'd learned to control. It had meant a lot to see my hard work come to something new.

Looking briefly at Zephyr and Sen, and knowing they were with me every step of the way, I began my tale of how Erlan had discovered someone was leaking information about me and possibly the Sanctuary to someone unknown. How Erlan had found the organization and identified a symbol the Sanctuary had banned.

There were murmurs from the council members as I told this part, but Vestan lifted his hand to encourage them to keep listening. I gave him a subtle nod and continued, naming the group.

I told them how we'd discovered who it was and that I'd intended to get to the bottom of it, hoping it was a mistake until I'd developed my third element.

This caused a stir. Martyl's eyes went wide, and Elowan dropped leaves to the floor. I moved on, speaking about the conversation Chris and I had had and my resultant refusal to entertain the idea of opening a portal.

"I don't know the history of Tuviel and Azargad very well," I said to finish, "but I trust Zephyr with everything, and he assures me that opening even one portal would be a very bad idea. I understand the Sanctuary feels the same. Rest assured, I have no intention of doing so."

"Thank you. All three of you," Vestan said as he got to his feet. "You've stood as a line of defense for us for some time now. You once again have our gratitude. The memory of the dragons is said to be incredible and respected. I am grateful you once again speak with wisdom and understanding and respect for the difficult times that came out of the last openings."

I listened as the council talked between themselves for several minutes after this, most expressing their concern that Amcika still existed.

"From my understanding of Chris and the belief he held, many of them think there are others like us trapped on the other side, as we are trapped here. His wish appears to be born from a desire to unite the mythicals, but they wish to do so regardless of the danger," I said when it appeared they were going to brand Chris a traitor.

Sierrathen got to her feet a moment later.

"While I am sure most of the mythicals in Amcika believe this, there have always been those who hold the same opinion as the Dark One did. He believed all races to be inferior to the elves, to be enslaved, wiped out, or used for the benefit of the controlling race."

As Sierrathen said this, Sen came over to me and leaned against my leg. I noticed her shivering and her mind was in turmoil, so I picked her up and held her against my chest.

She turned sad eyes in my direction, and I reached out to her with my mind.

Although it wasn't the first time I'd seen glimpses of a traumatic event in her past, she'd never shared the full memory with me. She did now, showing me an elf in the forest she cared for pulling up trees, hurting wildlife, and causing mayhem in an attempt to build something or attack an unknown force.

Watching through Sen's eyes, I saw her running away, fleeing animals such as deer. A centaur ran with her. Beside Sen were other myconids and mythicals I'd never seen before. One of the myconids was running alongside Sen, an older, weathered-looking one. The myconid stumbled a couple of times, but Sen helped him to his feet.

A moment later, a branch smacked him, taking the mushroom-like top off his head and pinning him to the ground. Pain and anguish tore through me like a knife to my heart. I stumbled back, momentarily unable to breathe. Zephyr let out a deep roar and swayed, almost falling.

The council gasped as my vision cleared and so did the pain. I realized Vestan was on his feet and I was being supported by a cushion of air.

I looked at Sen, tears coursing down her cheeks, and realized both why she'd never shared the memory with me and wanted to now. When one myconid died, the others felt the pain, and they did again every time they remembered it.

Pulling her closer, tears slipped from my eyes. She'd suffered when one of her kind had been killed by an elf like me. It made me wonder how she'd accepted me so readily.

Aella protect, Sen replied immediately, showing me the clearing where we'd met from her memory and point of view. Zephyr was behind me, with the dwarves and elves we'd been escorting to the Sanctuary at his side.

I sighed, knowing at that moment, I had shown her I wasn't like the elf who had murdered the myconid beside her.

Standing again, I nodded at Vestan, acknowledging that he'd caught me, then I reached for Zephyr and ran my hand over his scales. He moved closer, bringing his head down to Sen's level so he could lean in and let her know he cared too.

Although it was a vulnerable and intimate moment, it didn't feel wrong to be having it in the middle of the council chambers. Their words had triggered it.

"Forgive me," I said. "Sen was showing me an old memory, one with significant pain. It was relevant to your concerns. I assure you, we don't intend to let anyone enslave any race, mythical, human, or normal creature. We'll stand in the way of anyone who tries it."

I'd started speaking with tiredness to my voice, but by the time I finished, my anger and determination showed. One fist was clenched so tightly that my fingernails were digging into the palm of my hand.

"Then you offer us more than we could ask for," Sierrathen said as she stood again. "It's clear this breach of your trust is not something you will bear lightly. Were it discovered six months ago, we would be moving our home once again to ensure our safety. As it is, we must hope Chris wishes us no ill will and keeps our location to himself."

"If he doesn't, I am sure we can prevent any harm from coming to the mythicals here," I replied. "I'm happy to check in with you daily and work with Ronan to continue to assure the safety of the Sanctuary."

"Then there is nothing more to be done or discussed now. We will trust the processes we have and monitor known portals. In the meantime, I think it would be right for us to celebrate. I imagine there are at least two elves who are going to be delighted to discover you can control water."

I grinned as the corner of Sierrathen's mouth twitched up. Gwaelon and Ruehnar were likely to be delighted. It helped to have something positive to focus on, but I still felt an ache in my chest as the council meeting adjourned. I walked out with Zephyr and Sen.

My myconid was still very subdued and I continued to hold her close to me, hoping to provide her comfort. Her sadness when she thought about family had been explained, and it was awful. The three of us truly were bonded, each of us having come together after being alone.

We'll never be alone again, I said to them. *I'm going to always be with you both.*

Sen snuggled against me as Zephyr nuzzled me with his head. Warmth spread through me. This was my family.

Feeling calmer and eager to see the water elves before we found somewhere to sleep for the night, I made my way to the area of the Sanctuary where they were most likely to be. In that section, the nearby streams had been diverted and pushed into a new river, as well as several natural pools along the way.

It ended in a beautiful waterfall that was tall enough to look impressive. However, it had a deep pool and a low enough flow that it wasn't too loud.

And it was so tucked away you could hear it when you were close. As we approached, I once again marveled at the design and the skill of the earth elementals who had created this wonderful layout.

It didn't take me long to spot Gwaelon. The elf was sitting by the edge of a pool, reading a book and smoking a pipe. On the nearby rock wall were several sconces, ablaze with a steady flame that didn't move in the breeze. They took me by surprise, but I soon remembered I was in a magical place.

As I came closer, I considered splashing Gwaelon with the water from the pool beside him, but I was too worried about the book to do so. He looked up and saw us approaching.

"Aella, Zephyr, Sen, I didn't know you were in the Sanctuary. Did you come to see the treaty signed?" he asked, closing the book and getting to his feet.

I marveled at how quickly the elder elf moved but didn't say anything as he came down the winding path toward me.

"We didn't, but by luck, we were here to see the humans off. I admit we came for other reasons, one of which might interest you." I grinned as I finished speaking.

He studied me for a moment as if he was considering asking but trying to work out what I might mean first.

Slowly I reached out for control of the nearby pool and raised some of the water in a tall column. It was tough to hold it in one place, but it caught the elf's attention. His eyes lit up and he clapped in delight.

"Oh, my, I knew you'd get there eventually. I've known since that first day we put out those fires."

"You have?" I asked, puzzled by his response.

"Yes. You probably don't remember, but when I got there, it felt as if someone had been trying to lift the water out of the field below to use it to put out the fire. I checked with Ruehnar afterward. No water elves had been near there. It could only have been you. In the pressure of the moment, you'd begun to control water."

My mouth fell open as Zephyr chuckled.

"Why didn't you tell me?"

"Because I didn't think you needed the pressure, nor did I want to place responsibility on your shoulders before you were ready to accept it. You are Henera, and people will look at you differently the more elements you control. You are ready for three now, but you weren't ready for two then."

I frowned. I was not sure I liked that he'd made that decision for me, but I suspected he was entirely right. Back then, it had been hard to control one element, and I'd had Knox to deal with. I also hadn't begun to win over the Sanctuary until recently.

It might also have meant we never met and bonded with Sen, Zephyr pointed out.

Then I'm glad things worked out the way they did, I replied.

"Anyway, come, the three of you. My brother will be pleased to hear about your ability. Bialan is going to be so cross. He hoped that having Erlan and Seth spending so much time with you, you'd master fire next. Of course, it means he's lost his little wager."

"It sounds like you made that wager with inside information," I replied, although I didn't have the heart to be upset about it.

Feeling lighter and grateful for the friends I'd made in all sorts of places, I followed Gwaelon to find the other elven masters.

CHAPTER EIGHT

I stifled a yawn as I sat down next to Gwaelon and focused on the large bowl of porridge I'd been given. Sen was sitting on the table, her drink finished and a small biscuit in her hands.

Gwaelon had yet another book out in front of him, but he was flicking through the handwritten pages as if he was looking for something.

"What's got you searching?" I asked as I finished a mouthful. Behind me, Zephyr was chowing down on something large and meat-based for breakfast, and I grinned before giving the elven master my attention again.

"I was trying to look up some information on the whereabouts of a great heirloom of Ornthalas. He had a ring. It was said it helped him feel one with the water and call it from farther away."

I nodded, thinking of the bracers and necklace I wore. Every time I'd developed a new element, I'd been gifted with something that had aided that element. Something my ancestors had wielded.

"As with the other great heirlooms, it can only be activated by someone descended from Ornthalas, but it has been lost in time."

"I'm sorry," I replied, feeling disappointed for both of us.

"It will not elude me forever," the elf replied before patting my shoulder. "One day I shall see it grace your hands. It is the least I can do to aid in what might be coming."

A frown flicked across my face as he walked away. I could hope nothing was coming, but equally, I knew I couldn't be entirely sure either. I was slowly getting pulled into plots and schemes.

After two months of living without any issues and with no one left hunting me, I didn't want to return to the constant tension of before. Something made me sure I wasn't going to get my way, however.

There had been a look in Chris' eyes. I wasn't done with his group or what they intended.

After breakfast, we dropped in briefly with the other masters. I didn't stay with each long, most congratulating me before I quickly moved on. Zephyr also seemed eager to leave since he never liked walking much, and Sen was still subdued after the memory she'd shared the night before.

I tried to encourage them both, but it was clear that what we needed most was to return to the warehouse and have some time to fly and be ourselves again.

The thought of having to help Minsheng through his grief as well made me feel as if I didn't entirely want to return to my home, either. As much as I wanted to support him, it wasn't going to feel right at the warehouse while we adjusted to the difference in Chris being there or not.

Still, I couldn't hide from it in the Sanctuary, and I knew Zephyr and Sen needed me. Within the hour, we were in the skies again, flying to our home in LA.

It was strange flying during the day now. We'd spent over a year being so careful, and now we waved and smiled at people, flying lower than before and stopping off for snacks halfway through.

We were served with a smile, Zephyr hanging out at the entrance of the store while Sen bounded along the aisles, grabbing her favorite packet of chips off the shelf and then jumping up to deposit them in my arms.

Many shoppers laughed and pointed at her antics, and it brought out the mischief in her. She bounded onto the trolley of a mother, a toddler in the seat at the front.

The kid squealed with delight as Sen ran along the handlebar, then jumped onto a nearby shelf. A moment later, she handed down a package from a top shelf to an older lady too short to reach it.

I smiled to myself as I picked up Zephyr's favorite snacks as well, making sure to grab a couple of the largest bags they came in.

By the time I had everything we wanted, Sen was on my shoulder, smiling and waving at people again. I hurried over to the checkout, finding one of the larger conveyors empty and a smiling woman waiting to run my stuff through the checkout.

I noticed her eyes go wide as she spotted the myconid, but I gave her the best smile I could, as did Sen, and she grew more curious than scared.

"Are you one of those special people?" she asked as she beeped through the second item.

"An elf?" I replied.

She nodded and kept flicking her gaze toward Sen.

"Yes. I'm a mythical," I said before introducing Sen and talking about us and what we could do. To demonstrate, I floated my goods up into the air instead of bagging them up while I paid.

It drew me some looks, but it was a simple trick for me these days. When you could control the air around everything, you could control everything in it.

I felt lighter at heart as I made my way out to Zephyr, finding the dragon giving rides to some kids in the parking lot. He stopped as I approached, and we shared our snacks as I answered more questions.

Finally, we were done and continued toward home, but we'd been in the air for a couple of minutes when I noticed some resistance to my air control. Zephyr wobbled as he tried to compensate, and Sen wriggled down into my jacket to get out of the sudden blast of air.

A moment later, it happened again and I lost my grip on Zephyr's back, coming off for a moment before I could blast myself into place.

What's going on? Zephyr asked.

I'm getting...interference, I replied. I felt as if my control of the air wasn't complete. As if someone else had beaten me to it.

Want me to land? Zephyr's voice was full of concern and a desire to understand, mirroring my own.

No, try flying higher. There might be a wind elf practicing down there.

It was all I could think of.

Zephyr either agreed or couldn't think of anything better either because he rose, trying to put distance between us and whatever was happening.

No sooner had he done so than I felt something try to take the air around me out of my control, smacking into my grip on it as if I'd been mentally slapped.

For a moment I lost control, then I reached and pushed out whatever mind had tried to take it from me.

At the same time, torrential rain hit us, coming from seemingly nowhere. There were no clouds in the sky.

We're under attack by mythicals, Zephyr shouted.

I blinked, still wrestling with an unknown force while Zephyr darted from side to side, clearly trying to get us out of the rain and into a better situation.

Not sure what else to do, I tried to push everything out from us, taking control of anything around me that was water or air. I could feel the sudden attacks as other elves tried to pull at my control and blast me off Zephyr's back.

They're not attacking me, the dragon said a moment later. *Just you.*

My blood ran cold as the realization hit me. This must be Amcika. There was no other reason for other mythicals to be attacking me.

I wanted to cry at the brutal way I was being challenged. Nothing had prepared me for this.

Nothing.

Despite that, I did my best, taking back control of the elements as it was taken from me and doing everything I could to keep myself on Zephyr's back.

I was more worried about Sen, but she had the sense to tuck herself deep in my jacket and hold on tight.

Still flying here, there, and everywhere, Zephyr continued to try to shake whoever was attacking me. A moment later, a blast of air hit me and knocked me sideways. At the same time, I felt the air around me snap out of my control again and into someone else's.

I fell, unable to prevent it.

Zephyr raced after me and grabbed my arms. The three of us panicked until Zephyr dropped me into a bush just feet from the ground. I tumbled, branches stinging me as they snapped. It was less than ideal, but I finally stopped and was mostly unharmed.

He landed beside me, his powerful body protecting me and looking for the threat as I got to my feet. We were in a forest, but it wasn't one I recognized. There was a clearing up ahead, and we were off to the side of a dirt path.

For a moment, the air onslaught stopped, although rain still poured down on us. Sen shivered against me, and I reached up to help hold her steady and calm her. At the same time, I tore open one of the snacks I'd bought.

While I ate, I reached out with my mind and took control of the trees and plants. If there were mythicals in this place with me, I wanted to know where they were.

It didn't take long for me to feel three elves coming my way from the other side of the clearing. Before they could reach me, I sent a shock wave through the ground. After knocking them off their feet, I strode in their direction.

I wanted to have a serious chat with whoever had batted me out of the sky without so much as a warning or an introduction.

*Careful, Aella. We've never faced other mythicals. It's not like
facing humans. They can come at you in more ways than you
can imagine.*

You're telling me. But I can control three elements.

And there are three of them.

I exhaled. Zephyr had a good point. There was also the
possibility they had the mythicals they'd bonded with, but I
couldn't feel any creatures nearby.

While they were getting up, I strode into the clearing.

They looked like any three young adults would in
America. They were dressed in jeans and sweatshirts, but
there were subtle differences in the ears and the light in
their eyes—and the way two of them pushed themselves up
from the ground by blasting it with air.

The third elf in the middle got up naturally. He was
stronger-looking than the others and a good few inches
taller. He walked toward me.

"You're coming with us," he said, reaching out at the
same time a jet of water darted out of a nearby lake.

"No, I'm not," I replied, blasting him off his feet with air
as I pushed the jet of water to one side and in their
direction.

I didn't move, focusing my abilities instead and taking
control of the plants behind the trio. Reaching into them, I
made the vines grow rapidly toward the three and pull the
two air elementals off their feet before they could regain
their focus.

That left the water elf. He appeared to have far greater
control over the element than I did, and he sprayed me
again. While I'd pulled the other two elves out of the way,
and they were trussed up well enough that they couldn't

come after me, it didn't stop them blasting me with air while the water came my way full force.

Zephyr moved in front of me, taking the brunt of the blast so I could get to my feet.

We should run, Zephyr said.

I wasn't going to argue with him, but I was worried about Sen. Inside my jacket, she still shivered.

Sen okay. We run, she instantly replied.

It gave me the confidence I needed.

Feeling for the air around Zephyr, I worked out where the water elf was and made the ground beneath him drop several feet. At the same time, I moved the plants holding the two other elves up and back some more, distracting all three.

Throwing up an air wall between them and us, I took off, sprinting into the woods. Zephyr was behind me and Sen was still within my jacket.

For now, I didn't dare fly, but I used the air to make myself faster.

As soon as I was in the trees, he took to the skies since he was too big to keep up. He flew above me and occasionally circled around.

Although I couldn't be sure where the elves were, I couldn't feel them coming after me. I relaxed, thinking we'd lost them.

No. They're still coming, Zephyr said a moment later.

I growled, not sure how they could be.

How far behind are they?

Several hundred meters, but they're slipping farther behind.

I glanced back, trying to see them, then opted to change direction and turn northward for a bit.

They changed direction too, Zephyr added.

Frowning, I tried to work out why. Could they feel me moving through the air the same way I could feel people?

I wasn't sure, so I moved between the trees, changed the air patterns, and pushed my body faster, running hard in the old direction again.

Still following. I think they can see you somehow.

But I can't see them, I replied, looking again.

Sen came out of my jacket and got up on my shoulder, acting as an extra set of eyes. I continued to use the air to run as fast as I could, dodging branches.

As I passed larger bushes or vine-like areas, I took control of the plants and grew them across the path I'd taken to slow them down.

I think that's helping, Zephyr said. A moment later, he swerved to one side as something blasted up at him.

They attacking you too? I asked.

Yeah. Air blasts. I'll be fine.

Although he thought he would be and was probably right, I was concerned. We needed to do something to discourage these elves from following us before my abilities ran out. I'd never been up against my kind, and I didn't know how strong these three were or what their stamina was like. I was also out of snacks.

Sen see, the myconid called a moment later. *Bird. Mythical.*

I blinked. It made sense if one of them was bonded to a creature flying after us.

Sen help, she said, then leaped off my shoulder into a nearby tree. *Aella run.*

Fear filled me at the danger she was in, but Zephyr

echoed her sentiment and promised to keep an eye out for her.

Knowing she could easily run as fast as me and at worst Zephyr could pick her up, I kept running, but both of them dropped farther behind me.

There was a screech, and I felt a flare of pain in one of my arms before Sen started bounding after me, the gap closing.

Nicely done, Sen, Zephyr said into both our heads. My body grew less tense.

Reaching the edge of the woods, I slowed as Zephyr flew in front of me and circled.

We've got a clear five hundred yards or so, he informed me as Sen came flying along a tree branch, then bounded down. I reached up and snagged her, pulled her toward my jacket opening, and set off toward Zephyr.

Pushing my abilities as hard as I could, I powered into the air.

Zephyr came up and under me, and I gave him as much of a boost as I could, pressing against his back to stream-line us.

I felt something try to take control of the air again, but it was weaker than before, and I was more prepared for it this time. I fought it, keeping the air tight around us. Zephyr flew faster than a dragon naturally could.

Fear gripped at me, and I expected to have the air pulled out of my control, but we kept flying, putting distance between us and the site of the initial attack.

I had no idea who had attacked us or why, but I'd never been so grateful to get away from anything in my life.

CHAPTER NINE

The warehouse coming into view was one of the best sights I'd seen in a long time. More welcoming than normal, it sat in the bright sunshine, the plants flowering and Erlan sitting on the roof. Newton was dancing in the sand with the rest of the fire salamanders who still lived with us.

I waved, instantly feeling a lot more relaxed.

Sen poked her head out of my jacket, and I stopped powering Zephyr along as swiftly. I was exhausted, but I couldn't rest yet. We needed to find Minsheng, and I had to tell him what had happened.

Sen ran through the building to find my Shishou as I tried to usher Erlan and the salamanders off the roof. A wave of tiredness hit me, and my vision blurred. Forced to let go of the air around me, I wobbled.

Caught by Zephyr, I didn't fall, but I had to stop for a moment.

"What's wrong?" Erlan asked.

"I was attacked," I said as Minsheng appeared, Sen on his shoulder. "Other mythicals. Tried to take me."

My Shishou rushed to my side and wrapped an arm around me, helping Zephyr guide me inside. Before I could do or say anything else, tears ran down my face.

I'd been so happy for the last few months since we'd dealt with Jacobs. It was the first time I'd been free to be myself and be out in the open, then Chris had brought a new threat to our door, or something else had, and I had been attacked again.

On top of that, I had been entirely unprepared for it. No one in the Sanctuary or at the warehouse had taught the elementals to fight each other. Having my control challenged had hurt in a way I'd never experienced, and I felt like the frightened girl on the run I'd been when Zephyr had first hatched.

The difference was that I wasn't supposed to feel like that. I was supposed to be the strong one. But three elementals had entirely overwhelmed me.

It took me some time to calm, Erlan telling Daisy and the others in the warehouse what I'd said in the meantime. Daisy and Holfin did as they often would in stressful situations and made sure everyone had enough food and drink, then we sat in the kitchen together.

Although I still felt strange, and my mind kept going to the feeling of being slapped each time one of the elves had taken control from me, I tried to tell them what had happened on the way from the Sanctuary.

Minsheng got to his feet and paced, clearly concerned, but he didn't say anything until I was done.

"It sounds like Amcika," he said. "As much as I wish it

wasn't. There's no other group of mythicals that would do something like this. I think we're going to need to report this to the police and the Sanctuary, however. If they've grown bold enough to attack you in broad daylight, we should see what we can do about making sure you're safer from now on."

I gulped at Minsheng's serious response. Was I going to have to go back to being frightened of leaving the warehouse?

Erlan shuffled closer and put a hand on my shoulder.

"We'll work out how to beat them," he said, his eyes meeting mine. "You're the strongest mythical in existence. You've got some training to do."

His vote of confidence helped, and a hug from Sen added to the warmth.

He's right, you know, Zephyr said. *You are a lot more powerful than those three elves were, put together. It's going to take some practice, but then they'd never be able to come close to you.*

I hope you're right, I replied, feeling tired in my depths. So tired I wanted to go to bed and never get up again. When would this end?

It was a wake-up call if nothing else, and I took several deep breaths as I tried to calm myself and focus on what I was going to do next.

"We should contact your liaison at LAPD," Minsheng said. "Get him to come by. They'll want to know there are mythical criminals we're going to help them apprehend. Then you should talk to Ronan while I tell the organization."

Having clear direction, I got to it. I sent my contact in

the LAPD a message and let him know he might want to come to the warehouse. Then I headed to my room to connect with the communication stone. Zephyr and Sen came with me, and the three of us were sucked into the mental chamber with Ronan.

The centaur came closer as soon as he noticed us.

I told him everything that happened, grateful the council member never once interrupted me but let me tell my story the way it came out. It was easier a second time, but I still didn't manage to tell it without choking up a couple of times.

No sooner had I finished than Ronan stepped forward. He placed both hands on my shoulders and tilted his head forward until our foreheads touched.

"I am glad you got away and are safe with your Shishou," he said. "I will inform the rest of the council that it appears Amcika is on the attack, and we'll discuss what we might be able to do to aid your safety. The elemental masters might have wisdom in this situation."

I nodded, grateful the strong centaur was taking it seriously and thinking of ways they could help. It also made me feel better that his thoughts were leaning in the direction of helping me stay safe rather than the Sanctuary withdrawing or hiding again.

Feeling calmer and leaning into Zephyr for more comfort, I cut the connection. For a moment, I remained leaning against Zephyr, his head beside mine and Sen on my lap.

They were shaken too; that much was clear. I was grateful for how they'd stood by me, doing what they could to get me out of there too. We were a team, and it made me feel a lot better to know it.

Sen reached out one of her twig-like hands and placed it on Zephyr's scaly nose before putting the other on my arm. I smiled down at her and sent waves of gratitude and love toward both of them. We were a family. As strange as that was to others looking in. And someone had threatened our family.

Feeling stronger and ready to begin doing something about the attack, I got to my feet and helped Sen onto my shoulder.

Sen fight, she said, her little face stern underneath the mushroom-like cap.

I nodded at her. Yes. Whatever this Amcika were going to throw our way, we were going to fight. Before we could find Minsheng again and discover if the organization was going to help if they could, there was a knock on the large front door.

With it being too early still for the dojo to be taking classes, there was one person it could be—our LAPD liaison.

Hurrying to the door and grateful when Minsheng came with me, I opened it with as much force as I could muster and tried to look as if I wasn't concerned about who was on the other side.

Neil had a folder under one arm and his car keys in his hand.

"Feller in the office said you had something urgent to discuss and to get my ass over here as soon as I could."

"You could say that," I replied as I backed up and ushered him in.

Once more, he greeted Zephyr and Sen as if they were other humans, and we made our way through to the kitchen. Daisy had been baking since I was last in there, and the room smelled like cookies.

As we sat down and I started my tale for the third time, she fished the first batch out of the oven and plated them, then put them in front of us without asking us if we wanted them.

It gave me something to focus on, and I was still feeling the need to recharge my batteries, especially if I was going to be training later.

Neil listened as well as he had done the first time, making me feel calmer and better about what happened by being there. After all, he had a badge and was a police officer, even if he was also supposed to be asking me for advice on how to handle these sorts of things.

"Well, that's a new problem, no mistake. I must admit when they tasked me with talking to you about policing mythicals, I didn't think our first case would be someone attacking *you*."

"No, me neither," I said, unable to suppress a shudder.

"It's not going to make it easy to police this. If *you* can't apprehend them..."

"They were trained to take on a mythical like Aella," Minsheng said, coming to my aid. "And there were three of them against her. That they didn't succeed with those advantages is a pretty clear indicator that Aella is far more powerful than they are together."

I wasn't sure I agreed. I still felt strange after having my control of the elements attacked so forcefully, but I wasn't about to argue with my Shishou in front of anyone or insult his intelligence. I also appreciated his vote of support and belief in my abilities. Right now, I felt as if I were far weaker than I'd realized.

The attack had been a wake-up call. I might have grown strong, but there were still plenty of mythicals out there who, combined, could easily beat me. I kept wondering what would have happened if there had been one more of them. Or one of them had been an earth elemental as well, and I'd have had to fight on three fronts.

"That might be true," Neil said. "But it doesn't help me decide what to tell my superiors. They're going to want to know how to apprehend those three."

"We can provide a team of elemental elves to help take them down. And other mythicals are willing to help. They can be beaten. It just takes...different tactics."

"Okay, I'm all ears."

"How about we show you?" I said. "We've got many elves here now. Multiples of most elements. Why don't you stick around for training, and we'll go over some of what we're capable of?"

Minsheng raised an eyebrow but didn't object, and that got Neil's approval.

"All right," he said, standing up. "Show me what you're truly capable of."

I tried not to smile too broadly. Despite being scared of the other elementals and feeling less sure of myself, in the dojo, I was comfortable. There I had shown my abilities many times.

Neil happily followed me while looking around at our setup. It was clear he was the type of person who took everything in and filed it away for later. Part of me was worried he would see something that would lead to an advantage, but I reminded myself that I was on the same side as him now.

Admittedly, not everyone in the country agreed yet, but we were working on the rest of the people who still thought we were strange and different.

We found Emily and a couple of other elves in the dojo, the three of them working on something I couldn't see very well as I came down the steps. Zephyr flew down, going over the side to give everyone else more room, and it made me wonder when we'd reveal to anyone but the few who already knew that he could take human form.

Not everyone in the warehouse knew, but it was likely Amcika did. It made me wonder if we should keep something like that a secret from our team when our current enemy knew.

Before I could begin to decide, we reached the dojo floor, and Sen bounded over to Emily to see what she was up to.

The water elf was with the others around a strange-looking machine in a tub of water.

I'd have asked what it was, but it was identical to something I'd seen the day before. Another machine Chris had made.

"We're trying to make sure it does what Chris said it did," Emily explained when she saw my raised eyebrows.

When she noticed the police officer with me, she backed up, and her gaze darted between Minsheng and me.

I explained to her the plan, deciding that it would be a good idea to involve Emily in our demonstration. She could still control the water element better than anyone else in the building.

Over the next half an hour, we made a spectacle of our abilities. I made a tornado and moved it in a circle around the floor, doing my best not to pick up anything important and break it.

As quickly as I'd made it spring up, I forced the air to calm again, and it died. But if Neil's eyes had been widened with this display, it was nothing compared to his shock as Erlan joined Emily, Zephyr, Sen, and me in showing Neil what we could do.

Sen was the last to stand before us, her body focusing on the targets Ronan had set up for us to use in target practice. I expected her to release spores or something similar, but instead she put one foot in a puddle of water on the floor and stretched her arms toward the targets.

At first nothing much happened; the puddle was absorbed by her body. I waited and watched, pretty sure this was something new and more than ready to believe in the small dryad.

Sen attack, she said, and I could see her delight. Before I could ask what she meant, she flexed her arms.

Tiny ice darts hit the target, each one aimed so that she would have gotten a decent score on an archery target.

Neil and everyone else clapped as she turned and took a bow, her face alight.

I reached for her, and she bounded onto my shoulder. I started to wonder what else my bonded mythicals were going to be able to do as I gained more elements. My new ability to manipulate water was the sole explanation I could think of, especially given the look of shock on Minsheng's face.

"Well, you can do incredible things. I can see some good defenses, but we've got a lot of work to do."

I nodded. Neil wasn't wrong. Most of all, I had a lot of training to do. There was no way I was letting mythicals get the better of Zephyr, Sen, and me ever again.

CHAPTER TEN

Several days had passed, most of them spent training in the dojo or with the police helping them work through how to defend against this new branch of mythicals.

The Sanctuary checked in with us every day via Ronan's communication stone. They weren't happy about me telling the US government so much about our kind, but they agreed that we didn't have much choice. I also pointed out that they had plenty of data from the research they'd been doing on the mythicals we'd rescued.

I might be showing one man a bunch of what appeared to be magic, but he was doing his best to get a scared police force to cooperate with us.

So far, it seemed to be working. My cooperation had earned the warehouse a special line that allowed cops on the beat with mythical-related crimes to call us directly and get advice.

Zephyr, Sen, and I had also been enrolled in a training class. We were scheduled to go to the LAPD once a week and learn how to police safely and effectively.

Part of me was excited about it. The thought of helping people in the city I loved and becoming a force for good in a new way, along with my bonded mythicals, made me wake up with purpose. Since defeating Jacobs, we'd been happier, but we'd also been at loose ends.

We were on our way from our first session, one that had taken some of the shine off since we'd been made to read through ethics and code of conduct manuals for what had felt like hours, when I suggested we detour to the beach and enjoy the sunset.

Flying on Zephyr's back with Sen in her usual curled-up position in my jacket, I felt relaxed and at ease with my companions. We'd heard nothing from Chris and part of me missed him, but we were still in a routine and living life as best we could.

We landed on the beach, avoiding the majority of the crowd. I slid off Zephyr's back. Sen climbed onto my shoulder.

Please tell me our next police class will be more interesting, Zephyr said. I chuckled, wishing I could but having no idea.

Sen almost asleep, the myconid added, sending an image of her fighting sleep while I read the documents.

I didn't disagree with her, but I was pretty sure we weren't doing anything other police officers hadn't done before us.

Humans funny, she added, motioning with her small arm ahead of me and to my right.

I looked where she was indicating to see several young men, late teens or early twenties. They were wearing board shorts, and their pale bare chests were on display. They were running into the water until it was above their waists and then rushing out again, whooping in delight.

Shaking my head, I chuckled.

They're playing, I think, I replied. I'd once been a teenager that full of innocence and lack of care, but I felt lighter for seeing their antics. At least, until one of them stopped, suddenly limping.

He called to the rest and they went over to him, questioning what had happened.

I didn't hear his response, a blast of water knocking me off my feet. At the same time, I heard Sen squeal. Pain flared in my shoulder, although I was sure nothing had happened to it.

Zephyr roared as he came to me and blocked the jet. I scrambled up, wet sand clinging to my clothes. Sen ran over as the pain receded, but I noticed a dent in her body as if something hard had hit it. I grabbed her and tucked her inside my jacket, hoping it would offer her protection.

My blood ran cold as I whirled to face whatever Zephyr was shielding us from, intent on helping him. Five mythicals stood on the shore not far from where the teenagers had been. The boys had been blasted into the water.

I watched a couple struggling as the water around them churned and knew if someone didn't intervene, they were going to drown. I reached for the water near them and found another elf in control of it.

I smacked the control away, and the blast toward Zephyr lessened, and the female elf on the right-hand side stepped back as if I'd physically slapped her.

Before she could snatch control away from me, I pulled the water away from the flailing young men and lifted them out of the way with air. Moving as fast as I dared, I dropped them on the sand, both of them coughing and spluttering. I nodded at their worried companions as they gathered on the beach. Several of them glanced my way.

Then I turned my attention to the rest of the mythicals. They'd blasted us with water again, and Zephyr was beginning to weaken under the barrage.

Feeling little challenge to my control of the air, I blasted it away, spraying it out to the sides. At the same time I rocked the ground, trying to swallow the elves with the sand.

Before I knew how else to help us, several of the teenagers ran up and shoved the elf blasting nearest them. She went down and the pressure eased, but one of the mythicals in the center of the group stepped sideways, coming into my view on the side of Zephyr.

I recognized the elf. He'd been the ringleader of the group who'd tried to claim me before—another water elf.

Before any of them could react, I blasted him with air. It knocked him to the side, but he somehow used the water in the sand to steady himself.

A moment later, he drenched the humans trying to help me. I blasted the water away from them before something else knocked me off my feet once more.

Not sure what else to do, I scrambled behind Zephyr and tried to work out a plan.

Message Minsheng, Zephyr said. *We can hold them off, but we're going to need backup.*

The dragon's words calmed me. His ability to face battle and not panic was a quality I didn't have in the same way.

Sen burrowed deeper into my jacket, clearly scared this time. As much as she loved the beach and playing in the water, she was never as easy here as she was in her native environment, and we were being hit pretty hard.

On top of that, I could still feel a dull ache in my shoulder from the wound she'd taken, and I was starting to get other aches from the pressure Zephyr was under.

Despite the precarious situation, I did as Zephyr suggested, using my cell phone to tell Minsheng I was under attack and where I was in as few words as possible.

Part of me didn't want to involve the other mythicals in this fight, but I wasn't ready to handle this alone. And I didn't know what else to do. Feeling Zephyr stagger toward me as more pain flared inside us, I threw a shock wave out through the ground.

It bought me a fraction of a second. I tried to grab control of the air and water I could reach, and I hurled it at the mythicals in front of Zephyr.

Several of them reeled as if they'd been hit before I pummeled them with air and water, but they soon recovered. The central elf's gaze fixed on me, and I felt them trying to take control while water from another source blasted toward us.

Zephyr, gas, I thought as I tried to come up with something that might aid us.

The dragon slipped back as I threw up an air barrier, determined to keep the water and air we were being hit with from dissipating his breath weapon before I could make use of it.

He exhaled and I took control of that as well, moving a

small cloud of it toward one of the weaker elves before they could react.

At the same time, Zephyr ran at the line of five elves, his body scary enough they stepped back, eyes wide. Distracted by him running at them, I managed to envelope one in the gas cloud.

She tried to run out of it, but I followed her with it and used the air around her to slow her down. I felt someone try to snatch control of everything, but Zephyr roared and knocked another elf over, giving me the opportunity I needed.

The elf went down, and the humans nearby were freed from the water onslaught they'd been facing.

A moment later, Zephyr bellowed again, and pain flared in my hand.

I looked over to see that one of the elves had stabbed him with something in the front left paw. The blade was so sharp it had cut through his scales.

It was a lucky hit, he sent. *Went between scales.*

Still, it was clear it hurt. I crouched and hurried underneath his body to blast the elves again and check how badly he was hurt.

Want me to pull it out?

Yes, but—

Pain flared in both of us again as I yanked it out, trying not to twist it or make the wound worse.

Holding it in one hand and keeping a mental grip on the air barrier around us, I faced the elves again. There were four still standing, most of them as covered in sand as I was. The nearby humans had backed off, clearly not wanting to get involved.

"Why are you doing this?" I asked. "Why attack your kind?"

"You know who we are and what we want," the lead elf said, sneering at me.

"Amcika?" I asked.

One of the girls chuckled.

"You're not as bright as everyone makes out, are you?" she said.

Feeling my dislike of the elves in front of me grow, I stepped forward.

"I won't help anyone who is willing to hurt or kill innocent people. It doesn't matter what you want," I replied, so much anger inside me that I worried about what I'd do with it.

"You clearly don't understand what we want." The guy spat on the beach. "Humans are like rats. They infest everything when they are allowed to keep breeding."

I growled and moved to blast him off his feet with another jet of air, water, or sand, but Zephyr's voice stayed me.

Buy time, he suggested, which made me stop. *We have backup coming, and they probably don't.*

Although Zephyr was right, and it made more sense to talk to these four until our help arrived, it took all my self-control not to attack while I had a good opportunity. I was pretty sure at least one of the other elves before me was feeling similar, but whoever the elf in charge was, he held out a hand, and we continued to stare at each other.

"I've been ordered to take you in alive at any cost. If we have to kill that little dryad sheltering in your jacket, we will," he said.

"By who?" I demanded, surprised that I was being offered this much information.

"Why don't you come with us, and you can find out?" He stepped forward another pace.

I frowned, gritting my teeth and trying to decide how best to respond. I didn't want to go anywhere with these elves. I didn't get a chance to ask any more, however.

There was the sound of sirens from the streets behind us, and they were coming our way. It appeared Minsheng had called the human cavalry. At least, I hoped so.

The mythicals' eyes flicked in the direction of the noise.

"What do you say?" he asked. "Will you come and let us talk to you somewhere we won't be interrupted?"

"Anything you want to say to me, you can say here," I replied. "I'm not leaving this beach until I'm ready. But by all means, explain what's so important about me helping you."

The guy snarled, and I felt him reaching for control. I fought back, concentrating on holding the box of air around us and nothing else.

This signaled to the others that our reprieve was over, however. Within seconds we were under full attack again, but I didn't budge from my stance, holding our small area of the beach safe and us within it.

Now that I had some experience with other mythicals trying to take control of the elements I was manipulating, I found it easier to keep them from smacking my focus out of the way and replacing it with their own. They still tried, however.

A few times, I staggered physically as my body reacted to the blows my mind was taking. It was the strangest sensation, as if I was defending against someone boxing with me but in my mind. In this case, several someones with multiple elements.

The cops soon appeared, guns out and pointed at the mythicals challenging us. I was grateful to see Neil as he came closer, his eyes on the mythicals.

"While it isn't illegal for mythicals to practice their abilities in public," Neil said, locking eyes with the ringleader, "I have a feeling Aella, Zephyr, and Sen here aren't enjoying this and want you to step down. And I'm under orders to give her backup if she believes anyone is a threat."

The mythical laughed.

"You? You and your little human weapons think you can hurt us?" the guy jeered.

"With my help, they can," I replied, keeping my voice as calm as if I was pointing out a fact, not threatening him. "And he's right. I think you should stop and leave before anyone else gets hurt or the humans you drenched decide to press charges."

He scowled at me, and I felt one of the others try one last time to take control of the box of air I was using as protection, but no sooner had she gotten control of one small section than I grabbed it back so hard and fast that she staggered several feet and her nose started bleeding.

Easy, Zephyr said. *We'd be hard-pressed to keep everyone alive if they attacked, and I can feel you running out of energy.*

Zephyr was right, but more cars pulled up, doors opening and slamming. I glanced past Zephyr to see Erlan, Emily, and Ascan run up, with Minsheng, Jinto, Daisy, Grim, and Justin not far behind.

Newton and several of the fire salamanders scurried

across the sand with them and they stepped into the gaps between my feet and Zephyr's. They burst into flame, bright colors swirling among them as they hissed.

As Erlan came closer, he created a flame ball in his hand. Emily and Ascan reached for control of the water in the sea, bringing up a large funnel of it and threatening to sweep it sideways over the mythicals.

That turned the tide. They might have been able to beat me, Zephyr, Sen, and the cops, but with another three elementals and the extra backup, they were outmatched. Especially since my team was fresh, though I was exhausted.

"This isn't over," the guy in the center said, focusing on me. "You *will* come with us, even if we have to choose our moment carefully."

I didn't respond, fearing he might be right. I was unwilling to show anything but the strength I needed him to believe I had.

Without another word, the guy used his wind powers to get everyone in his group into the air, and as a unit, they flew south.

I relaxed, wobbling as exhaustion hit me. The fight had nearly drained me of power. I looked at everyone who had shown up to defend me and burst into tears.

CHAPTER ELEVEN

Another day dawned, and I tried not to show my fear. So far I'd been attacked two days in a row by mythical forces, and I'd barely begun training to defend myself against other mythicals.

After the attack the day before, I'd needed to eat and rest before I could do anything, but then I'd made sure Minsheng pushed me hard in training for the rest of the day.

When Zephyr had needed to catch me as I got dizzy and almost lost my connection with him and Sen, I admitted I'd done enough for one day. Zephyr had then insisted I rest and stayed with me, although Sen had taken an interest in helping Lyra with dojo classes in the evenings and learning things.

I was worried Sen was taking the threat personally, given she'd hidden in my jacket for most of the fight, but it was nice to get some alone time with Zephyr.

He'd switched into human form, and after making sure I was okay, he'd tucked me in bed and wrapped his arms around me. It had been pure heaven after a day of hell, and I didn't want to think of anything else, but we needed to get up and face another day.

I rolled over and found him awake, his warm body muscular and strong beside me.

"How did you sleep?"

He looked at me as if he'd just noticed I was awake.

"Well enough," he replied, "But I'm worried. I think we need to be extra careful with these mythicals. They seem dead set on having us help them open the portals."

I sighed. He was right. Zephyr was always right, but I wasn't sure I needed reminding about that part as well.

"We'll train. Might be time we stop hiding your abilities," I replied. "You're pretty effective with the elements as well. Might make them think twice about attacking us."

"No, I think we should keep it to ourselves as long as possible. They have Chris' word for it alone. If he told them."

I frowned but nodded. There was no way I was going to argue with Zephyr about it. For one, it was his secret, but secondly, he also had the extra strategy, wisdom, and understanding his genetic memories brought with him.

Sighing, I got out of his way so he could morph back. I'd begun to get used to seeing him in both forms finally, but it always took me a moment to adjust when he switched. Within seconds I had a full-grown dragon curled up beside me instead of a human that at a second glance didn't look right.

You could never tell what wasn't right when Zephyr was in human form, but he was almost too perfect. His skin was also somehow still bulletproof.

Once we were decent and ready to face the day, we made our way down to breakfast. Daisy or Holfin had left out waffles, and I added fruit and cream to mine while laying some out for Zephyr as well. He wolfed his down quickly while Sen bounded down from the shelf she'd been sitting on while she had a drink.

Sometimes I wondered what Sen thought of Zephyr and me being romantically involved as well as bonded, but she never said anything about it, and today I was more concerned that she was well after the battle.

I picked her up and set her on my shoulder, knowing she liked to be there and wanting to make her feel safe.

Sen want armor? I asked, having a brainstorm. Zephyr's scales had been made into a partial suit of armor for me. I'd not worn it since the last large battle I was in, but Minsheng had brought it up the day before.

If Daisy could design a smaller set from the small scales Zephyr shed, we might be able to protect her better. Then she'd feel more like part of the team.

Sen have Zephyr scales? she asked, her little eyes lighting up.

I nodded, grateful for the idea, and made a mental note to ask Daisy if she thought it was possible as soon as we got a chance.

With that in mind, the three of us went to find everyone else and get on with our day. We didn't have much in the schedule, but I wanted to train more, and I knew I needed to get better at controlling water and larger amounts of it.

That meant going to the beach. I had a feeling Minsheng was either going to insist on coming or bringing the others.

It took us a while to find everyone. Most were out in the alley by the back entrance. That door was rarely used these days, more of a fire escape than the route we'd once defended from agents trying to capture or kill us.

We'd come a long way from being barely able to defend the building to having the capacity to turn it into a fortress.

I hadn't told anyone yet, but I'd also begun building downward as a way to test my earth abilities and stretch them. I was being extra careful and taking instruction from the earth master at the Sanctuary so I didn't break the foundations of the building or make it collapse.

It took a long time to terraform the land you were standing on, but so far, it was proving useful. I was reminded of it and the secret it was when I saw Minsheng and the others gathered around something I didn't recognize.

They stopped when they saw me and I walked over to them, aware that Zephyr couldn't get more than his head out the door in his current form. They had a device spinning in the breeze, but it didn't seem to be working properly.

"What is it?" I asked as Minsheng looked at me.

"Another contraption Chris made. It was supposed to power the building and help keep us safe from things, like an elemental-powered shield. A bit like the defensive one the Sanctuary has, but one that would stop people passing through the border it creates."

I blinked. Why had Chris never mentioned it?

Probably because it's not working yet, Zephyr projected, answering the question I'd not asked aloud.

It was a good point. Chris tended to tell us about things

that worked or ones he needed us to test. Otherwise, he beavered away in his little space, making things. Now he was gone, and his designs had been left behind in their varied states.

Minsheng clearly missed him. He walked over to me with a sad light in his eyes, the spring gone from his step. Not sure how to comfort my Shishou other than be there for him, I gave him a brief smile and stayed put.

"We should get your training going as long as you promise not to push as hard as you did yesterday," he said, giving me his attention. "We'll return to this another time."

I saw Daisy and Jinto relax. They had been tinkering with the contraption. Between them, they wheeled it inside, and Minsheng headed for the area of the large room where his desk was and where we normally started our training.

Emily and Erlan were not around. I wondered if I'd somehow missed them and asked my Shishou.

"They've gone to the beach to train some more."

Minsheng raised his hand as I opened my mouth in surprise at the pair taking such a risk without me.

"Before you object, they've gone to one of the busier areas where there will be plenty of witnesses, and I've instructed them to call Neil and us the second there's a sign of trouble."

"I'm not sure that's enough. Those five came out of nowhere yesterday, and it was three the day before. They shouldn't be going out there without Zephyr, Sen, and me for backup."

Minsheng came closer and put his hands on my shoulders.

"I know you want to protect us all, but I'm pretty sure Erlan and Emily are safe. These people are clearly after you for what you can do. It's you they're risking the wrath of the mythical community for."

I wasn't sure how to respond to that. It was clear that Minsheng was right, but equally, I wasn't sure it was safe for the others without me since there was a threat to their lives while they acted as my backup. No matter how I tried to explain my reasoning Minsheng seemed to think they were safe on the beach.

Zephyr came closer as we talked about it and nuzzled me with his head.

Aella.

I turned toward him, feeling so many emotions I didn't know how to respond.

Minsheng might be right. They seem set on taking you, not anyone else.

But what if they take one of the others as bait or attack them to make me weaker?

Then we'll get there in about three minutes flat. The determined firmness of Zephyr's words made me feel better. The beach wasn't that far away. It wasn't as if we had a long way to go, and Zephyr could fly fast when he needed to.

Okay, I said a moment later, trying to let go of the fear and worry.

Erlan and Emily were also growing stronger. With the practice they'd gotten in the warehouse beside me for months and the experiences we had, they had honed their skills faster than the elves at the Sanctuary.

Relaxing, I turned to Minsheng.

"We'll train here for a bit, then I'll go join them," I said.

"No way," Minsheng replied, his turn to object. "It's not safe."

I took a deep breath and thought about the best way to explain it to Minsheng. In the end, I could think of one good way of putting it.

"No one here can hold their breath long enough for me to fill this place with water and then empty it again, and I wouldn't risk your lives. If I'm going to keep training and growing my skills with water, I need to control larger amounts. We get that at the beach."

Minsheng opened his mouth to argue further but closed it again. I wasn't sure if he was going to think of something, and I didn't want to stop him from having the opportunity to speak his mind, so I waited.

"You make a good point, but for the same reason you didn't want Emily and Erlan going to the beach, I don't like the idea of you three going without us taking sensible precautions."

I nodded, expecting that. Of course, it helped that Emily and Erlan were there. I would have immediate backup.

"Okay, everyone," Minsheng called to those still in the building. "Looks like we're going on a beach trip. Bring that device. Maybe we can get it working better out in the open with a bit of help."

I nodded, grateful for the company and amused that Minsheng was being as protective of me as I was of the others. It was a good thing. We cared about each other, but it was clear we had a lot of safety elements to think about again, and we needed new strategies.

We'd hidden in darkness before, but I had no desire to

do it again. I wanted to be out in the daytime, and it was time for the mythicals to be in the light in general. If we wanted humanity to trust us, we had to do our best to put ourselves out there and show we could help.

After spending an hour in the dojo with Sen and Zephyr working on combined skills and things we could do together, some of the others packed up the van and got it ready to take a bunch of stuff down to the beach.

I grabbed more snack bars and drinks than I would normally take with me. It was one of the few ways I could prepare for a third battle with the strange mythicals trying to kidnap me.

I should have been used to not knowing what might happen by now, but this was a whole new level.

Do you remember many of Tuviel's fights with the mythicals? I asked Zephyr when we were about to leave.

Not many. My memories are of Azargad, who spent a lot of time as a dragon. When he was in human or elf form, he had one element to control, and he could fly. It made far less sense for them to battle any other way than as a pair, especially since there were no cities like this or buildings she would go into where he couldn't fit.

I sighed, sensing Zephyr's frustration. Our lives were nothing like our forebears, but I got the feeling their lives had been simpler in some ways.

More complicated in others. They were never allowed to be together the way you and I are.

Good point. I looked at the large dragon, and his eyes met mine. I felt warmth spread through my torso as I looked at him. I loved him. I'd have done anything for him and couldn't have bonded with a better mythical.

Grateful for every day I got to spend knowing who I was and grateful for the moment I found his egg, we flew toward the beach. Our friends followed in the van, and it wasn't long before we were on a stretch of LA beach.

Now all we had to do was stay safe and make sure no one opened portals to a possible hell dimension.

CHAPTER TWELVE

It didn't take us long to find Emily and Erlan. The sea was acting strangely where Emily was controlling it and keeping it calm for little kids to bathe and splash. Erlan was having fun cooking a spitted roast for another group of humans.

I found myself grinning. Zephyr landed, and Sen and I slid off his back. The two elves had created a party-like atmosphere on the beach, using their abilities to help others and create some fun. It was magic of a whole new kind.

Feeling left out, I took control of some plants near the shore and started growing them, shaping them into beautiful displays. When I spotted kids trying to make a sandcastle that kept falling over, I reached out and helped them, putting the sand together and pulling water up from the wetter levels below.

I earned cheers of delight when the sandcastle stayed in place.

Another kid noticed and made a request for help with

his project. I was soon building an entire sandcastle from scratch, modeling it on an English castle I'd seen on an educational video as a teenager while Zephyr stood beside me and kept me shaded.

I grinned up at the dragon when I was finished. I'd made another kid happy. He rolled his eyes, but his mouth was open in a similar grin.

By then, Minsheng and the others were out of the van and on the sand with their stuff, including the strange device. It felt odd bringing something experimental out in the open when the beach had so many people on it, but if the beachgoers were worried by it, they didn't show it.

With the sandcastles made and Zephyr stretching his wings in the sky above me, I walked down to join Emily. She was still holding the water steady, making it easier for the younger children to play in safety.

Reaching out, I felt her control of the element. Taking care not to accidentally steal it from her and hurt her, I tried to find the bits she didn't control.

In the year she'd been learning in the dojo with Minsheng, she had come a long way. I could feel her control as she moved from some particles to others, letting the sea she manipulated move and waves come through the area, but moving with them and guiding them.

It was a lesson in and of itself, and I was stunned as I felt it.

Although I'd been controlling the water for days, I was excited about getting to her level. It was an amazing skill.

Moving farther up the beach, I tried to mimic her actions on a small patch of water. It wasn't as easy as she made it look. For several minutes I struggled in vain, getting tenser. It didn't seem to be working.

Erlan came closer, the barbeque he was helping with done. He placed a hand on my shoulder.

"You once told me that there's no forcing our abilities. That we're supposed to join with the elements we command. You're trying too hard."

I exhaled, remembering saying something like that during one of our lessons. In truth, Minsheng had once said something similar to me, and I'd simply passed it on. It felt weird hearing it from someone else, but he was right. I'd needed reminding.

Taking deeper breaths, I refocused and felt for the water as if it were an extension of myself. I felt it moving back and forth, the water rolling over itself each time a wave crashed before flowing out again.

This time I managed to calm it by redirecting. Gently at first, and then with more control, I copied what I'd felt Emily doing.

A grin spread across my face as the waves before me died down and I created my patch of calmer water. I hadn't been there long when Minsheng came to stand beside me, his face alight.

"I still can't believe I get to see you do things like this," he said. "You've come a long way from the frightened young woman trying to push paddles and lift bowls."

My Shishou's praise made me beam. Progress was good, and having a way to win over the locals was better. It wasn't long before I was calming the water for more kids.

Some of the parents looked on, concerned it would come to an end and the elves standing on the shore would stop controlling it. Sen bounced around in the water as well, and when Erlan and Daisy joined them, it made everyone braver.

I held it until Zephyr landed beside me, a concerned look on his face.

We might be needed farther up the beach. Someone in trouble out to sea. Riptide.

"All right, I'm going to slowly let this area return to normal," I called, making sure everyone playing heard me.

Thankfully the swimmers reacted quickly, and the last few people in my area moved to Emily's. I noticed hers had shrunk since she'd first begun, but she widened it again to accommodate the extra people.

I gave her a nod as Daisy came up to me, her eyes searching mine.

"Zephyr says someone is in trouble farther up the beach. We'll go help them and come right back," I said, taking control of the air, ready to fly as I mentally called for Sen.

She bounded onto my shoulder, then slid down into her usual spot in my jacket. There was no way I was leaving the little myconid behind if this was likely to be a quick rescue.

While Zephyr flew us closer, I considered if Emily would have been a better choice, but she couldn't get there as fast, and I was pretty sure it was important for us to hurry.

Flying north up the beach, Zephyr headed straight for the trouble he'd seen. Once again, I marveled at how far he could see. The person in distress was a long way up the beach, beyond the main section, and the lifeguards were too far away to get there, although several were trying.

It was the perfect opportunity for us to show mythicals could help, but we had to hurry. I used my abilities to help us fly faster, worried the person might drown before we could help.

Zephyr flew straight and true, and we were over them in a minute or two. Swooping lower, he helped me get close enough to reach for control of the water. The water was too choppy for Zephyr to be sure he could pluck the man out of it.

It took me a moment to get control of everything, but I soon had the water stabilized, finding it easier than I'd expected to. I frowned when the sea seemed to calm on its own, but I lifted the guy up.

Getting air under him and the water off wasn't the easiest of tasks while flying circles on Zephyr's back, but eventually, I held him above the waves, and we moved to the shore.

As the lifeguards reached our section of the beach, I landed him on the sand. Zephyr circled again while we waited for the lifeguards to check that he was okay. He was conscious and looking our way, but it wasn't until one of the lifeguards gave us the thumbs-up that I felt we could retreat.

We'd barely flown a hundred meters when I felt a jet of air blast into the side of my body, knocking me off Zephyr's back. Instinctively holding the air around me, I steadied myself until I was flying over the sea beside Zephyr.

Those mythicals are back, Zephyr said as he flew up and over me. I headed to shore as fast as I could, getting ready to land and defend us against whatever was coming, hoping the people we had helped would consider helping us.

More air and water battered me and I felt a mythical trying to take control. It was all I could do to keep flying in a straight line.

You okay? I asked Sen as I dropped onto the sand with a bump.

Sen safe, she replied as Zephyr landed beside me and let out a roar so loud it almost made me deaf.

Get farther up the beach, he commanded as a shockwave ran through the sand and almost knocked me off my feet.

More of them? I asked as I wrestled for control of the air around us as well as the ground beneath my feet.

Yes. This was a trap.

I blinked, my blood running cold as I looked at the guy we'd rescued. He stood, the lifeguards who'd gone to his aid half-buried in sand and struggling to get free.

Another shock wave rippled through the ground as he smirked and came my way.

Feeling drained, my pack with Minsheng and the others, I panicked. We couldn't fight this many of them alone and spent.

Despite this thought, I knew I had to protect Zephyr and Sen, if nothing else.

I closed my eyes, trying to find some calm inside myself, then I latched on to the air around me and the ground beneath me again.

Exhale, Zephyr, I thought, but he was flying toward the elf on the sand and puffing out.

I could feel one of the other air elementals trying to control the gas, but I focused on it and pushed away the control, making sure it surrounded the mythical on the shore before anyone could stop it.

It engulfed the lifeguards as well, an unfortunate consequence of them being too close, and I felt guilty. I was knocked off my feet, too distracted to see the next hit coming.

Zephyr roared again, but I was blasting myself to my feet, the ground stable enough for that. I'd dealt with one of the mythicals, but my dragon was no sooner by my side again than my attackers landed south of me on the beach, blocking my route to my friends.

There were still five of them, but I was low on power and my head was pounding.

"We're getting tired of asking, Aella," the same spokesperson said as a van pulled up on the road nearby.

Another couple of mythicals got out, and my heart sank. I was pretty sure there was no getting out of this. I was beaten, and they were going to achieve whatever they were trying to do.

We could surrender, Zephyr suggested. *It might buy time.*

Maybe. But... I frowned, looking at the mythicals.

A moment later, I slumped my shoulders, making it look as if I intended to do that. As if I were beaten.

All five of the mythicals on the sand with me walked forward, grinning their faces off at having won. With my mind, I reached for the air between us. None of them were paying attention.

Without hesitation, I blasted a wall at them. At the same time, I grabbed the sand and opened it, swallowing them as the other mythical must have done to the lifeguards.

All five struggled in the sand. Sen squeaked in delight,

and Zephyr roared. I packed it in around them, moving everything until they were held tightly. Several times the air elementals tried to blast air at me again, but I kept a wall around me, and Zephyr was solid enough that he could withstand it.

By the time I was done and the five were trapped, my head was throbbing, my abilities spent.

I was about to turn to the two elves by the van when I felt my control slipping on the air around me.

I've got nothing left, I told Zephyr as I let go of the air barrier around me, not wanting to risk losing our connection as I had once before.

I'd not been able to feel Zephyr or Sen, and both had panicked, not to mention that I'd been lost in the forest and had struggled to get out because Zephyr was always my compass when I wasn't with him.

We've got this, haven't we, Sen? Zephyr replied as the dryad pushed her way out of the top of my jacket again.

The small myconid jumped down and ran forward as Zephyr half-ran, half-flew toward the two. I watched Sen blast small ice darts at the elf closest to her. He swatted them away with air, but she fired so fast that some got through.

Zephyr tried to attack the other and breathe gas his way, but the mythical could move pretty fast and appeared to control earth. Every time Zephyr got close, the ground shifted and either blocked the attack or moved the elf out of the way.

I exhaled, trying to work out how best to help them, but before I could move, I felt a sting at the back of my neck. I whirled as I reached up and pulled a dart out, then locked eyes with another mythical—a man I recognized after two years.

A man who had once stolen my hairbrush and led me to Zephyr's egg stood feet away on the beach, not far from the mythical who had faked his distress and the lifeguards I'd knocked out with Zephyr's breath weapon.

The gnome-like mythical held a dart gun, and he shot me again. I tried to get control of enough air to defend myself, but I didn't get enough together before a third dart hit me. Then Zephyr was near, roaring, but I felt fuzzy. I had no idea what I'd been hit with, but I was pretty sure it was too late.

Aella, stay awake, Zephyr called, but I couldn't seem to form thoughts to reply.

I was aware of yet another elf, his long hair shining in the sun as he stood over me and what sounded like another roar from Zephyr before I could process that I was lying on the sand looking up.

When Sen appeared, her concerned little face near mine, I tried to smile at her. I felt light and as if nothing mattered, hopeful it would be enough to calm her.

CHAPTER THIRTEEN

The first thing I was aware of was the pounding in my head, then movement. I was in what felt like a vehicle, being driven somewhere at a fairly high speed.

"She's coming to," a voice said, familiar, but my mind was too foggy to think where from.

I tried to open my eyes, aware of Sen near me and Zephyr flying above. When I finally managed to make my eyelids respond, I found I was blindfolded and my hands were tied.

Given my abilities, I wasn't sure what good it would do them, but I wasn't going to make it obvious what I was capable of. I might need the advantage later.

While I laid there, I tried to think about what I remembered happening and why I was in the situation I was in. Zephyr helped remind me, his body still flying somewhere above.

Where are you? I asked in my mind, confused about his lack of being near me.

In the air above the van, they have you and Sen in. They

tried to trap me in a net, but I got a claw through it and ripped it off. They've let me follow you for now.

Where are we going?

South. I think we might be in another country now. They crossed what appeared to be a border. Well, they went under it. I was worried they were going to keep you inside, but you came out of a tunnel in a desert and kept going.

I exhaled, my heart racing at the news. How long had I been out?

Most of the day. It's beginning to get dark.

My thoughts went to Minsheng and the others. They must be worried about me.

Trying not to panic, I reached for the air around me, not taking control so much as working out where it was and who was breathing and moving near me. It felt as if there were a small army in the van with me, possibly all the mythicals who had attacked, but I couldn't be sure.

It was enough people that I didn't like my chances of getting out of the van, especially since my head still throbbed. Although I'd been resting for a significant amount of time, I'd not eaten or drunk anything, and I was pretty sure I wouldn't be at full capacity.

If need be, I'll take human form and get you out, Zephyr said.

I'm not sure we can beat them combined, I replied. *And I'll need you to be a dragon to fly me out of here.*

Good point.

Sen help, the myconid said, the first indication she was awake. I reached for her with my mind and tried to soothe her.

She sighed and moved closer until her head was resting on me, the weight comforting.

"You sure she's awake?" someone asked.

I fought not to react and instead breathed calmly and in the same steady but shallow way I thought people did when they were out cold, although I couldn't be sure they were buying it. No one said anything for what felt like ages.

With no idea what else to do, I continued to rest and tried to talk to Zephyr about what he saw. Slowly I grew sorer, my body objecting to being tied and bounced around. Either from exhaust fumes or apprehension, I also felt sick.

Despite the times agents had chased me and the people who had wanted to kill me over the last few years, no one had ever come close to kidnapping me and taking me from the people I cared about.

When Jacobs had imprisoned me in his compound, I had made it easy for him to do so and not tried to escape. I was genuinely stuck now and had no idea how to escape. It was terrifying.

We'll get you out. I promise, Zephyr said.

I reached for him, wishing he was closer but aware that wouldn't help how I felt. He was farther away than I'd have liked. At the same time, Sen wriggled again and made me aware of her nerves. I tried to calm her as Zephyr tried to calm me, and onward we traveled.

Time blurred, my mouth growing drier as it passed and my stomach feeling emptier and emptier. I didn't normally go this long without food. My abilities demanded a higher calorie intake than the usual person's.

When I could stand it no more and Zephyr and I agreed there was a chance I'd be offered something if they knew I was awake, I moved.

"If she wasn't awake, she is now," someone said as hands reached out and grabbed one of my arms.

I flinched, but it got a good grip, and there was a sharp sting in my arm. A moment later, I relaxed as a sedative rushed through me. It wasn't enough to knock me out, but it made it hard to focus.

"What was that?" I demanded, the words coming out slow and slurred.

I tried to think of what I wanted to say, but it was hard to get my mind to focus, and no one spoke or answered my question.

"Food. Water?" I asked, blinking beneath the blindfold.

There was a chuckle from somewhere in the vehicle.

"We're not that stupid," a woman said, coming to one side. "We know that eating and drinking more makes elven abilities stronger. You're going to have to get used to being hungry until—"

"The boss will tell her what we want her to do. She can wait until then and not before," a gruff voice interrupted.

Silence followed as I tried to focus enough to use my abilities. I wriggled my fingers and found they were numb, the bonds on my wrists having put them to sleep. It was a place to start freeing myself, but I tried to reach for the bonds around my wrist with my mind to unravel them, the rope something I should have been able to control.

It didn't respond to my attempt for control, and a moment later, I moaned when someone slapped me.

"I wouldn't try to do that either," the woman said. "It

won't work while I'm controlling it. You aren't strong enough to beat me on an average day, let alone while you're partially sedated and starving and you depleted yourself recently. You might as well chill out and accept that you're staying in here until we decide otherwise."

I exhaled, not sure how to respond to such a statement. My cheek hurt. This was an entirely new situation for me.

Sen help, she said, shifting against me.

"And I wouldn't let that dryad attempt to undo your bonds if you don't want me chucking her out while we're driving. I have no qualms about putting the length of your bond to a test."

Sen, better stay still, I replied, not giving the cold woman confirmation I'd heard her. I didn't want to have either of my mythicals too far away from me. It was bad enough that Zephyr was flying above the van and was not in it.

Not sure what else to do, I waited and hoped my head would clear. Minutes into this decision, I wondered if my new abilities might help me. I'd had a liquid injected into me. Was it possible for me to take control of it and separate it from my bloodstream?

That's got to be the sedative making your brain think crazy thoughts, Zephyr said.

I almost laughed aloud but managed to stop myself. It was a crazy thought, but I'd seen water elves heal and keep other elves alive by pushing on the blood flowing out of a wound. As long as I was careful, I was pretty sure I couldn't make it much worse.

Closing my eyes and trying to ignore my discomfort, I reached into my body with my mind. It was resistant to the intrusion. Almost as if my body were trying to defend itself, it tingled everywhere I tried to connect and attempted to rebuff my mind.

At the same time, I could feel the flow of blood and other fluids in my body as they moved or were sent rushing by my heart. Not sure where to begin, I spent minutes getting familiar with the major organs and making sure I wasn't doing them any harm.

Then, very carefully, I tried to work out what the sedative felt like and how I could encourage my body to filter it out of me. Nothing was obvious, however. While I was aware of the different elements in my bloodstream, it was nothing like controlling water or connecting to the waves in the ocean or the water in a bottle.

Eventually, I had no choice but to give up and hope my faster elven nature took care of it before the people I was with realized it had worn off.

The rest of the journey either flew by quickly or we reached our destination not much later. The van stopped.

You've been driven into a cave in the side of a mountain, Zephyr said, who had been left behind. The knot in my stomach grew worse, and it helped me focus. I tried to reach for control of anything around me of the three elements I could control, but something blocked each one.

"She's getting restless again," someone new said. "Trying to control the air."

A moment later I was slapped again, and the pain made me angrier. Whoever these people were, I wouldn't hesitate to attack them when I got a chance.

"If only her Shishou had taught her how to properly connect with the elements around her and make them hers permanently," the woman replied. "She's nothing special. Can't believe everyone thinks she's Henera. She's pathetic."

"We shouldn't get complacent," the gruff male voice replied. "No other elf can control three elements, and she's changed the minds of almost the entire world about our kind. Gone up against the US government. She has power, even if her use of it is crude."

I would have sworn at them if I had dared, but I wondered what they meant. What was so rustic about how I used my powers?

As soon as the van stopped, I tried to sit up. Immediately someone pushed me down and then bumped Sen, sending her rolling off me. She grabbed with her small hands as I growled.

"You'll stay there until we're ready to move you," the woman said as Sen climbed up to her perch.

Sen in jacket, I told her, not wanting to lose the myconid when the time came. I needn't have bothered since she moved closer to me and tucked herself in, burrowing against me.

Although I knew there was a chance the three of us could work together to get us out of this mess, I wasn't about to demand Zephyr start pulling apart an cave network to get to me. He was strong, but I wasn't sure he was that strong.

I'd try, he said.

I know you would, but there's likely to be a better way, even if it's you leading the others here to rescue me. We'll find a way.

I'm not leaving you in there. His response was instant, and I was pretty sure there was going to be no arguing with him.

Before I could think anything else, I heard the door on the van slide open. Someone grabbed my arms from behind and pulled me out of the van. I flailed, helpless and worried I was about to crash into the floor. Instead, several sets of hands steadied me and lifted me upright until I could get my feet under me.

I felt lightheaded, and I swayed while others kept me from falling. When I finally had my balance, all but one hand gripping an arm let go of me.

Sen see, the myconid said, showing me an image of the area I was in. The van had been driven into a cave and we stood near the center of a large cavern, the interior lit with strip LEDs and large lanterns hanging from the ceiling.

The cave had been turned into a workshop, with other vehicles beside the van and workbenches on the other side. Ahead of us was a silver door, the kind that admitted someone to an elevator.

I tried not to react as if I could see, not wanting the elves I was with to realize my bond with Sen gave me the ability to look through her eyes. That meant stumbling and shuffling along and moving only when led somewhere.

Thankfully no one seemed to be paying me much attention as I was ushered to the elevator and inside. I felt the rush as the metal box lifted, carrying me upward as Sen made sure I could see the panel with buttons on it.

There were three others in the elevator with me, wearing robes. I noticed the robes bore emblems, the symbols for water, earth, and air.

It was clear these three were the ones who had fought my attempts to control the elements, but none of them were the elves who had attacked me. That made sense. The elves who'd attacked me had drained their abilities; these were fresh enough that they could easily stop me from getting free.

It also spoke of something more important; this group was organized. And they were right. I wasn't ready for something like this. Despite having trained at the Sanctuary and with Minsheng, I had no idea how they could keep the grip they had on the elements so solidly while mine was broken with seeming ease.

As soon as the elevator reached the correct floor, I was pushed outward. I almost tripped over the lip between the shaft and the elevator. Thankfully, the hand gripping my arm held firm, and I didn't fall.

I was marched down a corridor, going past what looked like cells although each was different, and I was thrust into the one at the far end. It was made of plastic, white and uncomfortable-looking. Nothing but a box built into the heart of the mountain. I had a feeling this was one of those prisons designed to keep an elemental in one place.

As soon as the door slammed behind me, I whirled. The door was a combination of plastic and metal, each piece fitting together so precisely that I couldn't find any air pockets big enough to create pressure. It wasn't going to be easy to get out of here.

While Sen climbed up onto my shoulder and undid the blindfold for me, I reached out of the cell I was in, trying to find air I could control. Although I could feel the element out in the corridor, it was strange, almost solid, as if someone else were controlling it. I wasn't about to challenge whoever that was when I'd barely gotten here.

After Sen undid the bonds around my wrists, I reached

for the earth or any water that might be in the rock of the mountain I was in. Again I met with resistance; someone was controlling the earth outside the box, although I also had to go several feet in either direction before I could feel anything.

It was an insane setup. The thought that had gone into my prison alone scared me. All the details had been thought out; there would be no escape.

These people had been training to fight me while I had been training to fight humans. If I stood any chance of getting out of here, I was going to have to learn fast.

CHAPTER FOURTEEN

Sighing, I got to my feet again. I'd been in my prison for what felt like hours, Sen my company in the cell and Zephyr sitting outside on the mountain. He didn't dare relax either.

We'd spent the first hour trying to figure out how to release Sen and me. The next hour I'd flopped on the floor and tried to control the elements near me.

With my abilities still mostly spent, I had quickly tired of being so easily defeated and instead tried to feel around me and try to work out how far from the surface I was.

Zephyr had spent the third hour flying around the mountain and looking for another way in despite the distance between us almost breaking our connection. Of everything that had happened, this had made me grateful that the sect of elves hadn't tried to take my necklace or bracers. I was still connected to the mythicals I cared about most, although I wasn't sure the necklace and bracers couldn't be removed against my will.

It was our fourth hour. My body was letting me know I

hadn't eaten recently, and I wanted to either cry or hurl something large and heavy at any elf wearing a robe or otherwise getting in my way.

Not that I could, and that was worse. I felt powerless and helpless.

We'll get you out of this, Zephyr said again. *There's no way I'm letting you stay stuck in there. But it's looking like I'm going to have to take human form.*

No, I replied immediately. *They might know that you're capable of that, but the chances they know what you look like are slim. Chris saw you in human form once and briefly.*

There was a pause, and I felt Zephyr shift up on the mountain.

I think they're looking for me.

Avoid them if you can, and consider finding a hiding place nearby but not on the mountain.

You know I won't leave you.

I exhaled. He was right. I was sure there was no way he would leave me since there was no way I'd have left him if it was the other way around. That said, I suspected he might have to.

But I hadn't exhausted every possibility of a way out yet. No one had come to see me, but they couldn't keep starving me or denying me water. I would need sustenance if they wanted me to do something for them.

Deciding I'd had enough of being passive, I made my way to the door and banged on it.

"I'm getting thirsty in here," I yelled as loudly as I could. "And I want to chat to your boss about why I'm here."

There was no response at first, but once more I reached out to the air in the hallway and tried to control it.

Someone smacked my control away, but I felt a person move out there.

I was drained, but it gave me info. There was at least one elf guarding me, as well as elves controlling the elements around me.

They have to sleep sometime, Zephyr pointed out. *There's likely to be a window of opportunity.*

It was a good point and it made me tentatively reach out with my mind to see what I could feel without actively fighting with an elf for control. There had to be a lull as two elves swapped control, or a weaker point when an elf would be tired and I might be able to take advantage.

To find out, I was going to have to be patient, but I'd been here for several hours, and I was still in the dark about a lot of things. If Minsheng and the others didn't manage to find me and rescue me soon, I was going to have to do something to get myself out.

Banging some more, I called again, acting as if I didn't know anyone could hear me. There was still no response. What was it going to take?

Maybe they're busy? Zephyr said, his voice sounding forlorn.

Busy trying to catch you?

No, they appear to have given up again. It's getting dark, and there's a lot of mountain for me to hide on. I can also run faster than they can. There's not a lot they can do to me if they do find me.

I sighed, wishing the same had been true for me. I was also confused. They had left Zephyr and Sen alone. Of course, I was grateful they had, but I was also puzzled.

They were part of me, my bonded creatures, and there

was plenty Zephyr could do that I could as well. It was clear they had gaps in their knowledge. The woman in the car had bought into the lie I'd told that none of us could survive without our bonded creature being close.

Of course, we'd not tested it for long. It was possible it might break the bond if they were away from me for too long, but I wasn't looking for an opportunity to try it.

Knowing they weren't well-informed made me calmer, however. All I had to do was figure this problem out like any other.

After banging and yelling for the fifth time, I gave up and sat down again, focusing on resting to see if it would help my abilities come back. With any luck, it would give me a way out, and for now, it meant I could focus on sensing when the elves guarding my cell swapped.

More time ticked by and I felt myself dozing, so focused on the way the elements around me felt and the signature of the person controlling each of them that I didn't realize someone had come to see me until there was a clang and the door swung open.

I didn't move from my position on the floor but watched as a familiar face came into the room.

"Hi, Chris," I said, waiting to see what he had to say for himself.

"Hi, Aella," he replied. "Good to see you."

"Given the circumstances, I can't say the same."

Sen hissed from my jacket, anger coming off her in waves. I tried to send calming thoughts her way, not sure anger would help us and not wanting to expend too much energy. I noticed Chris had come alone, with no food or drink as far as I could see.

"So, are you the boss?" I asked when he stood there, not doing much of anything.

"No. I have a pretty high position, but I'm not in charge." He leaned against the wall by the door, surveying me as I surveyed him.

I waited for him to explain, deciding I was comfortable with silence and he was going to have to break it. It was petty, but I wasn't above petty.

"So, have you thought any more about my question?" he asked a moment later.

"What question," I replied without missing a beat. "The one where you ask me if I want dinner before I leave? Or if I'd like a drink? The answer to both of those is yes."

"Well, both of those could be arranged, but I know we're both thinking about whether you'll open one of these portals for us."

"And you know the answer to that. I won't do it, and you won't keep me here forever, either. If I did change my mind, starving me isn't going to help me open a portal. It sounds like I'm going to need to be at full strength."

"Oh, Aella. You've not worked it out yet, have you?"

I frowned, not liking the amused tone of Chris' words. If I'd missed something important, what was it?

Me, Zephyr said.

"Your dragon," Chris added, confirming my realization. "I mean, you could attempt it, I suppose, but it has a good chance of killing you with three elements. Zephyr, on the other hand...in human form he has your abilities, and he's practically indestructible. By virtue of your bond, he's far stronger than any elf. And you."

"Then..." I gulped. I was the leverage. They were going to use me to persuade Zephyr to do what they wanted.

I exhaled, trying to process the information. It made sense now why they weren't feeding me or giving me anything to drink, and I was entirely sure that was going to remain the case.

They were going to force Zephyr to cooperate with them by harming me, depriving me of food and water and who knew what else.

Chris straightened, drawing my attention as Zephyr sent waves of comfort my way.

"You know, it would have been a lot easier if you'd agreed to open a portal or two, but given you don't think it's a good idea, we need to make sure it happens. Then we can show you there was nothing to fear. Hopefully, there will be no hard feelings after that. There'll be other dragons and elves."

I shook my head, not buying his words. If I was wrong and he was right, there was no way I was going to feel anything but intense dislike for him and what he was allowing to be done to me.

I'm going to get you out, Zephyr said as Chris made his way out.

We'll get me out, I replied as I pushed up and rushed forward, taking control of the air in the cell and using it to make me faster. I was near the door Chris had gone through when something hit me from the other direction, blasting me back.

For a moment I fought it, trying to snatch control of the air, but I was forced out of it and pushed back. This wasn't how battles usually went for me, but I was drained.

Stop, Zephyr said. *You're going to need to rest and regenerate as much as you can. We'll get you out before anything else happens to you.*

All right, I replied as I gave up. *But promise me you'll focus on keeping yourself free and away from here.*

I'm not going any farther than I need to, but I'll stay safe. Until then, we need to plan to get you out.

There wasn't much I could say to this. I was tired, my body hungry and dehydrated. I didn't know how much use I was going to be if this continued, and it was going to get worse.

It was hard not to be angry. I'd been betrayed by someone I'd thought was safe and had my back. Someone who had helped Zephyr, Sen, and me stay safe on many occasions. Now it appeared he'd had an agenda of his own.

I had so many questions. There was the guy who had stolen my hairbrush and started everything. What did he have to do with this? Had he known Zephyr was there? Had that been a strange coincidence?

While I sat and tried to rest, Sen curled up against me, clearly feeling a mix of emotions. At the same time, Zephyr settled down in the shadows on the mountain above. It felt so wrong, and a thousand times worse than our stay in prison had been. There I'd had some control. I'd been fed, given the necessities.

On top of that, I'd had a clear plan to get out and a trial date. This time I didn't know what I was dealing with or who, and I had no idea when it would end or how much worse it would get before I was free.

As I dozed, too uncomfortable to sleep, I imagined all

sorts of possibilities. It got worse as the night continued and my cell grew colder.

On top of the mountain, Zephyr didn't seem to be faring any better. It was cold, and rain started at some point during the night. It was no good. We were going to have to find some way out of this place soon, if only for one of us.

Sen, do you think you could get us help? I asked her when I was awake for the fifth or sixth time.

Sen help, she replied, lifting her head. I hated having to ask her, but she was our best bet. They wanted Zephyr, and they were prepared to use me to get him, but they didn't seem to have much of a purpose for the myconid, almost as if the plan they'd made didn't take her into account. That meant she was more useful to us safe somewhere.

She was also the most useful to us not here. Admittedly, I wasn't sure how she'd get to Minsheng and the others, but she might not need to get far, just to another Shishou in the country we were in. The organization could probably do the rest for us.

Sen find Minsheng, she said as if she were trying to reassure me.

I sighed but nodded. There had to be some way of getting her out of the mountain. I had to find out as much as I could about our prison and buy us some time.

Bluff, Zephyr suggested. *You've got nothing to lose at this point.*

He wasn't wrong, but if I was going to make them think I had changed my mind or was considering it, I had to be convincing.

What do you know about the portals and these elves? I asked
Zephyr.

For a moment Zephyr didn't respond, then his deep,
calming voice filled my head. I listened as he told story
after story about his ancestors and what they'd experienced.

CHAPTER FIFTEEN

It was almost morning by the time Zephyr and I finished talking over what we knew. There were clearly gaps and memories that were fuzzy from the passing of time, but it made me feel more sympathy toward these elves. They had been cut off from another realm against their will, and they wanted to see if the people and ancestors they'd cared about had survived.

Part of me couldn't blame them for wanting that, but they weren't going about it in a way I agreed with. I planned on seeing if some attitudes could be changed. And if not, I was about to learn something.

After getting up and tucking Sen into my jacket where she could see but go unnoticed, I went to the door again and banged on it.

"Okay," I yelled loudly enough that I'd have woken anyone on the other side if they were sleeping. "Tell whoever you need to that I want to talk. If Zephyr or I are to open anything, I want more info."

There was silence, so I yelled it a couple more times and

then sat. I was lightheaded and my throat was parched, a dull ache in my head, but I would have to cope. I tried not to think about it, not wanting Zephyr to pick up on how I was feeling and worry about me.

I can tell you're hurting, remember. It hurts me too. And Sen. Zephyr's words made me wish I could shut him out and spare him, if only for a short while.

The elves knew exactly how to impact us. It was going to be hard to resist their demands and get out.

We can work out how to make sure this never happens again once we've gotten you out, but for now, don't worry about me. I can handle a headache, and from up here, I can see for miles. I'll know if the cavalry arrives.

I asked Zephyr to tell me another story—a happier one. I closed my eyes, trying to rest until someone came to us. I didn't know how long I'd have to wait, but I planned on conserving as much of my energy as I could.

Despite having not eaten or drunk, I felt better. My abilities were slowly getting stronger, not that I planned to do anything yet.

Time drifted past and I was pretty sure I dozed again. I heard Zephyr's gentle, soothing voice in my head each time I woke up. I wasn't sure if he stopped talking or persisted while I was drifting. I could tell he was lonely and was trying to shield me from his emotions, but as he could feel my pain, I could feel his anxiety and sadness.

Eventually, there were footsteps outside again. I scrambled to my feet, not wanting to appear to be in any hardship. I'd see what I could get out of this conversation.

The door swung open, and instead of revealing Chris or the gnome who had stolen my hairbrush, an elven woman stood before me. She was wearing a dress and a robe, the style almost medieval, and she had a circlet in her hair. It was clear she was a pure-blood elf, and from the lift of her head and the look in her eyes, I was pretty sure she was proud of it.

"You in charge?" I asked when she looked me over as if I were a mongrel dog.

I lifted my head as well, looking her straight in the face, determined not to be intimidated. Whatever I was, I was happy with it. I wasn't going to be made to feel any other way.

"I'm who you need to talk to if you have questions," she replied, her voice harsher than I'd expected.

"Awesome. I'd like to see a portal, and I also want to know what it will take to open one, and what you guys plan to do about what lies on the other side. All I've ever been told is they were shut to stop someone evil. I want to know why you think they're no longer a problem and what you plan to do about it if they are."

"That's a lot of demands for someone in your position."

"What position? You might have me in a cell, but you still can't open anything without Zephyr and me. And I assure you, he's not helping you unless we agree on it being safe enough no matter what you do to me."

The woman pursed her lips, looking me up and down again.

"All right," she said. "Come with me, and I'll show you what I can."

I exhaled and nodded, trying not to reveal the immense relief I felt. If nothing else, getting to see more of the complex would make it easier for me to escape or get Sen out. And more information was still going to be useful since I was pretty sure there was nothing this woman could tell me.

She led me out of the cell and past two male elves, one on either side of my cell. Sen looked around for both of us while I felt the elements, trying to work out who controlled what while also being as subtle as possible.

"I'm Aella," I said when the elves fell in behind us and acted like an honor guard.

The woman glanced at me, and I suspected I wasn't going to get a reply. Whoever she was, she didn't need to give me that information.

"You're descended from all four of the highest-pedigreed elves, yet you barely know what you could be capable of," she said instead.

"I'm learning quickly, I assure you," I replied, not sure I liked the scorn in her voice.

"Well, for your age, you're far behind what I'd expect."

"That's likely to happen when your parents decide to make you appear to be an orphan and hide you in a human family who have no idea you're not human. I found out I was an elf two years ago. I'd say my training is going peachy for two years, wouldn't you?"

She snorted in acknowledgment, and we stepped into the elevator. So far, I'd seen nothing but the floor of prison cells, but I was finally about to see something else.

We went farther up, heading away from the entrance I'd been brought in by, but I wasn't worried. It was giving me more information, and I had a feeling I could make this more than one conversation if I needed to.

"I'm Cherisse," she said as we reached the top of the shaft and she waited for the door to open.

I didn't speak, not sure how to respond to this info. Had I said something that softened her?

She might think she can influence you now that you've pointed out how little you know about the elven world and how little time you've been in it, Zephyr said. *She could be trying to be nice, however.*

I guess we'll find out either way, I replied.

This next floor took my breath away. It was built into the mountain, but the walls were mostly glass. There were windows to the outside everywhere.

Similar to the way the elves had lit the Sanctuary council chambers with mirrors, glass, and natural light, the elves here had lit an entire floor.

I stopped and looked around, struggling to take it in.

"It's quite something, isn't it? We could teach you to create buildings like this, you know. With your control of multiple elements, it's highly likely you'd be able to do this alone. After some practice, of course."

The offer sounded sincere, but there was an undertone of smugness to it that made me wary. Almost as if I'd given her yet another element of leverage. If she thought that I was going to be bribed by the offer of learning something I could probably figure out myself after trial and error, she was mistaken. However, I didn't intend to let her know that.

"This is one of the most beautiful places I've been," I replied, exaggerating.

Cherisse smiled, which I was pretty sure was a sign that

she'd made some of it herself. But there was no way to be sure, and I didn't plan to pry any further.

"So, why are we up here?" I asked. "Beyond how good it looks. I'm pretty interested in the subject of the portal and how one is opened."

"You don't want to know more about why first?" she replied, but kept walking, going deeper into the mountain.

"I figure the why doesn't matter if it's not something Zephyr and I are capable of yet. Let me know what we've got to do, then I'll know if I need to be persuaded." I followed her, feeling Zephyr shift on the mountain above as if he were trying to keep up with us and get as close to me as possible.

He was closer than he had been since we arrived, and I appreciated not having our bond stretched so far.

Be careful not to be seen, I said as he came closer. *There are a lot of windows here.*

I know. They've tried to hide them, but I've snuck past a few.

I was relieved. I needed Zephyr to stay safe if any of this was to work. I also needed to find a way to get Sen out.

Sen find, she replied, showing she was paying attention.

Onward we went, the area getting darker despite the light that was being reflected around. It was a strange part of the mountain with two of the walls rock, but it still had a beauty to it.

While we moved, Cherisse glanced my way now and then, but I tried not to meet her gaze. I pretended I was a lot more interested in the light and the way it was being directed than I was. If she wanted to brag and give me a good excuse to check out the exits, so be it.

At the same time, I gently reached out to see if anyone

was controlling the rock or air nearby. Although there was some control, and I suspected it was the three elves near me doing it, I tried to search beyond to find out what was nearby but out of sight.

The most surprising element was the stream running through the rock and that the elf who was controlling the liquids near me wasn't trying to control it. It wasn't easy to connect to and control water that was moving so fast, but Sen might be able to take it.

As we rounded a corner, I saw the rock in the very heart of the mountain open to a corridor on three sides of us. Ahead was another wall of glass, but something beyond that wasn't lit up in the same way. It was confusing, but Cherisse motioned for me to approach the glass. I had a feeling I was about to be shown something.

She stayed behind and moved to one side.

While I was peering through the glass, the light increased. The whole area was suddenly flooded with light, more mirrors directing it into the room beyond.

It was a large natural cave, and in it were three pillars carved with ornate runes. Between them was a platform with more patterns and swirls carved into it. Around it were the runes for the elements, and farther out were large boulders.

I stepped closer to the glass and felt tingling in my skin and humming in my ears. Not liking the strange sensation, I stepped away.

Cherisse laughed, making me jump.

"That is why we need someone who can control the elements. If you get too close to the portal and the stones that have been erected to prevent its activation, it pulls the body apart. Or anything else for that matter."

"All four elements are used to assault the body. If you'd gotten much closer, it would have tried to drain your blood out of your ears and nose and set a fire in your stomach."

I shuddered, not sure how I could combat that and live. I'd be fighting the boulders for control of myself while trying to break them.

We could do it together, Zephyr said.

But neither of us can control fire.

We don't need to. Dragons don't burn, not even an air elemental dragon like me. This is why they need me.

I bit my lip, terrified and curious about the challenge. A moment later, I eased closer, trying to anticipate the control the boulders reached for within my body by connecting with everything first.

It mostly worked. The pressure mounted as it tried to push me away, but I couldn't stand it for long since my stomach felt hot. Backing up, I exhaled and let go of everything. This wasn't going to be easy for Zephyr or me.

"Nice try," Cherisse said. "But it's going to take a lot more than that."

"Yeah, so it would seem," I replied. "Is there no other way? Can you not blow up the boulders?"

Cherisse raised an eyebrow. I couldn't tell if it was because my suggestion was awful or it had never occurred to anyone.

"It's an interesting idea," she said when she recovered. "We've tried several things, and I suspect it would do one of two things: the pillars would render the explosion inert before it could happen, or it would explode, and the pillars and the center of the portal would rip a hole in the dimensions and kill us all. Would you care to try it and find out?"

I shook my head. She had a point. Explosions could do unexpected things, but I wasn't convinced it would be that bad.

Looking at the pillar, I considered. There had to be more to this. I wasn't letting Zephyr anywhere near the portal, but now that I knew it was a challenge, I was curious about opening it.

While I was standing there thinking, a drop of water fell from a stalactite above. As it came down and passed between the pillars, it exploded into a cloud of steam, vaporizing a moment later.

My mouth fell open. I'd clearly been lucky not to have been blown apart, so I could understand why Cherisse didn't think much of my idea. This thing was chaotic enough.

"All right," I said as I turned to her. "Let's move on."

CHAPTER SIXTEEN

Trying to look around without being noticed, I followed Cherisse deeper into the mountain again, going down partway to the cell I had been held in but getting off on another floor. This one was lit more naturally, with lights, painted walls, and gorgeous carved furniture everywhere.

We passed doorways to offices and living quarters and what appeared to be a library. I walked in, awed by the number of books in the room when gentle lamplight revealed them. It was one of the most beautiful libraries I'd ever seen. The natural rock ceiling reflecting the light and polished to a shine along with the dark wooden shelving encasing leather-bound books that looked as if they'd seen centuries was so stunning I gaped.

The two elves who had been tailing me hung back and stood to either side of the library door, appearing to ignore us. I tried not to worry about them or make it obvious as I reached out to the air in the room and found that some at the far end wasn't in anyone's control. The elves here might be proficient at keeping connected to the elements, but their range wasn't as good as mine.

Cherisse walked over to one of the writing desks in the middle of the room, but I didn't follow her. Instead, I wandered closer to the shelves, looking at the titles. Most of them were in Elvish, but I had learned enough from Minsheng that I recognized some of the words. He'd have loved to be here since so many of them were about training in the elements.

There were also books on the history of many races and mythicals, and some human history. It was amazing.

"No wonder your elves are well-trained, with resources like this," I said when I finally went over to Cherisse.

"It certainly helps, but the elves here know what they're committed to."

"If you have so many powerful elves, how come they've not worked together to open the portals?"

Cherisse's jaw clenched and she looked away for a moment. I waited, not intending to make the moment any more comfortable for her.

"It's a lot more complicated when you need all four elves to be protecting all four elves. If one slips in the slightest—"

"Everyone dies," I finished, wondering how many powerful elves had been lost that way.

"It's against our code for anyone to attempt it without passing many other trials."

"Anyone you care about," I corrected. "If it was anyone, Zephyr or I would be doing those trials, wouldn't we?" I smiled as I spoke despite the anger bubbling up inside me, but my words came out with a lot more snark than I'd intended.

Careful, Aella. We need her to think we're at least interested, Zephyr reminded me, and I exhaled. At the same time, Cherisse looked down and relaxed.

"Actually, you have passed many of the tests our elves go through and shown great control in the other areas needed. Chris was confident in you after all the training Minsheng has had you do."

I blinked. Her words were an admission that Chris had been working behind our backs since the beginning and steering my training to teach me how to do this. But what did that give me that the others didn't have? Was I that much better at controlling all the elements at once than separate elves were?

It is extremely hard to do this, Aella, Zephyr pointed out. *I'm not sure either of us can do it, despite what she thinks.*

I wasn't about to disagree with my dragon. He had a point, though. Whatever this was going to take, we'd need to be rested and ready. There was no way I was going to let Zephyr do it alone, if at all.

"Okay, assuming Zephyr or I is capable of opening the portal, I want to know what you know about it and what lies beyond. I want to know everything about this evil elf on the other side, and I want to know why you think it's worth taking the risk. And finally, I want to know where you'll be if the elf everyone is afraid of does come through. Will you be cowering in a corner somewhere, or will you be standing beside me and trying to beat him back?"

"The latter," Cherisse replied, her voice firm and her

eyes lighting up with indignation. "I don't believe he has survived. Our kind might live a long time, but millennia? No. He's dead. But if he weren't, I would lead my elves into battle alongside you and be proud to do so, Henera."

My mouth fell open. That hadn't been the answer I was expecting, and it was almost enough to persuade me to consider her request.

But I knew I couldn't be that arrogant. I didn't get to take that risk for the billions and billions of humans and mythicals living on this planet. It wasn't my right, and neither was it theirs. Voicing that opinion right now might get me killed, however.

"As for the rest, let me start with the history of why they were closed and how it was done," Cherisse said a moment later. She strode over to a bookshelf as if she knew what book she wanted and pulled out a large leather-bound tome.

The spine was in Elvish and I frowned, hoping I wouldn't receive any scorn for not being able to read the language as well as a native elf could. I was tired of the animosity, and despite explaining I had grown up in the human world thinking I was human, I had a feeling she would still hold it against me.

Instead, she sat down and motioned for me to take a seat nearby.

Warily, I did so, and I deliberately fetched Sen out of my jacket as well, hoping it would give the myconid a chance to run around and find a way to escape if we needed her to. The elves guarded the door, but that didn't mean she couldn't stretch her legs.

Cherisse glanced at Sen but said nothing and flicked the

book open. She was incredibly careful with the pages, which were dry and yellowing, the ink faded. She looked at the text as if she were looking for something specific.

A moment later, I noticed a picture of the pendant I wore around my neck. With it were the bracers on my wrists and two more items, a ring and a belt or metal links that wrapped around the body. It wasn't clear.

"I see you have two of these," Cherisse said. "But you and the others in the organization probably don't know that the four great elves who wielded them used their power to close the great portal. Many other elves came together in a great display of strength to do the same at the lesser portals."

"There's more than one portal?" I asked. "And one of them is greater than the others?"

Cherisse raised one eyebrow before she sighed.

"You haven't been taught much about this part of our history, have you?"

"I'm getting the impression that you're the ones with the information," I replied without missing a beat. "The humans have taken delight in destroying information on us, believing us to be just that: mythical. And although the Sanctuary has some texts and prizes them highly, they've moved around a lot and haven't always been able to take everything with them."

"Then this might be a long lesson."

"If that's the case, may I request some water or food?" I asked. "I've not eaten or drunk in over a day, and while I suspect I'm faring better than a human would under these circumstances, I'm still suffering and will not be able to concentrate for much longer or endure the pounding in my head."

It was a lie, but I was pretty sure I'd delivered it well. Cherisse considered my request.

"Water I'll grant, but you don't need food. Zephyr will be making the attempt, not you. However, if you need information to convince him, we'll ensure you can absorb that."

It wasn't the answer I'd hoped for, but it was a start, and it would help me stay alive longer.

I expected her to have someone else fetch it for us while my guards remained, but she motioned for one of the elves at the door to go get it for us, leaving one to control the elements.

Although I didn't give any indication I'd noticed, I felt the connection leave the rock around us and noted the elf who controlled that element. It might not be much information, but it was better than nothing.

With that, Cherisse ran me through the process the elves had used to shut the portals, and how it would be a two-stage process to open them again. Zephyr or I would need to break the outer set of pillars to keep them from preventing other living beings from getting close. After that, an elf of each element would work together to open the portals.

"What if someone opened the portal again? What's stopping that?"

"Most elves can't get close enough," Cherisse stated. "And if they can, the pillars fight that as well."

I didn't respond, not wanting to inform her that I could easily get close. It made sense that most of the elves couldn't, considering what I'd witnessed so far. It had never occurred to me, but one of the ways I was more powerful than other elves was the range of my abilities. It made sense. Most of the time, range wasn't a factor.

"If that were possible, it would still be a waste of time and energy. No one could travel through them from this side, and anyone trying to get here would be incinerated."

"Okay," I replied, "Not a great idea."

Cherisse rolled her eyes and went back to the book. I followed her explanations about the history of the portals, but in my mind, I was processing. If the portal was opened and this evil elf still lived and was in charge, having him come through and be incinerated by the other runes might be a bonus.

Admittedly, if he was dead, it might kill innocent elves who were hopeful they could reunite with us. But it gave me more questions.

"Why can't they open the portals from the other side?" I asked when Cherisse continued to talk about it. "If the elves on the other side are related to us, why can't they solve this problem? How did any of this work to trap this elf who no one will name?"

Cherisse let an exasperated breath out as I interrupted her mid-flow for the second time.

"It's complicated."

"I need to understand if I'm to make this work for you, so I guess we'll have to go over it."

No sooner had I finished responding, knowing I sounded demanding but deciding I didn't care, than the guard returned with a jug of water and a couple of glasses on a tray.

Sen got up, eyeing the water, which reminded me she was probably thirsty too. The tray was put down on the table in reach, and Cherisse motioned for me to go ahead.

I grabbed a glass and lifted the jug, but instead of pouring myself a drink first, I gently tipped some onto one side of the tray. Sen bounced over and stuck her feet in the puddle. Cherisse stared, and I got myself a drink.

"Right," she said a moment later. "The other side of the portals is a world very different from the one here. While the elements are present and the world is beautiful in its way, it's not as...malleable as it is here."

"Why's that?"

"Over time, the elements remember the elves who controlled them. They become...difficult to hold onto. You will have begun to benefit from this in your building. The air there will be used to your control. The foundations and walls of the building will be more attuned to your presence. When you die, another elf will find it harder to control."

My mouth fell open as more puzzle pieces fell into place. I struggled to control the elements here because the elves here had been doing so for a long time. It was a home-field advantage. Some of my power was negated.

"So, because there haven't been elves here for a long time and there aren't many, the elements are easier to control and manipulate. And over there, this evil elf has far less power," I said, checking that I understood everything.

"Yes, that's one reason they can't open them. That, and the four great elves created a prison, capturing him in it here by using the greater strength they had on this side and then taking it into his world and spending a long time fixing it there. It's possible he died in it."

"But it's possible he didn't?"

"Yes, sadly. No one knows what happened."

"Right. I was led to believe there are elves or mythicals who want to free him." As I said this, Sen finished her drink and decided to jump down from the table. Thankfully, Cherisse and the others didn't seem to notice as the myconid explored the room.

"There are, but we don't tolerate those among our ranks. We may have been painted to be a cult or something far more sinister, but we just want to see our kind reunited and able to flourish once more. We're powerful, and we can make this world a better place. The mistakes our ancestors made with their world won't be made here."

"But this world isn't ours by the sounds of this. It belongs to humanity," I replied, processing what she said and not believing a word of it. The elves sent to capture me had made it clear they hated humanity.

"And what are they doing with it?" Cherisse demanded, her voice cold. "They repeatedly demolish the beauty around them when they should be protecting it. They tear it apart for profit and think it won't devastate them the way our arrogance led us to turn our world against us. We can stop them from making these mistakes. Stop them from wrecking their planet."

I frowned, my fists clenching as I tried to control the anger I felt. This had been an enlightening conversation, but it hadn't done anything to persuade me to help these people open the portals. They were arrogant, blind to the dangers, and cavalier about my health and life, as well as Zephyr's and Sen's.

Be careful, Aella, Zephyr said again, sending calmness my way to diffuse my anger. *I agree with you, but you're in a precarious position.*

I know, I replied. Sadness washed through me. We still had a lot to learn, but to hope to change this cult's mind was a fool's goal. It was clear my only option was escape.

Now I'd drunk something, I was feeling better. My stomach was almost painfully hungry, but the throbbing pain in my head and the rest of my body were diminishing.

All I had to do was make them believe I was considering it while I regained my strength.

"So," Cherisse said, breaking through my thoughts, "what do you say? Is this enough information to satisfy you? Do you understand why this must be done now?"

I tilted my head to the side, trying to look more thoughtful than I was.

"It's a lot to take in and think about," I said after a moment. "I'm going to need to talk to Zephyr, and I'll probably have more questions, but I definitely understand better than I did."

Cherisse studied me, clenching and unclenching her jaw a couple of times. I was pretty sure she'd hoped I would be more yielding than this, but eventually, she nodded.

"Fine. We will take you to your room now, and we can talk more tomorrow."

"Understood, though I'd appreciate a toilet break along the way if that's possible," I said, scooping up Sen. The myconid had returned to my side once we began wrapping up. "There's a distinct lack of plumbing in my room."

For a moment, I thought Cherisse might refuse, but she gave me a curt nod and motioned for me to follow her.

Hoping to see more of the building and eager to get a moment alone, I hurried after her. This had been progress, but I was still very much trapped and at their mercy.

CHAPTER SEVENTEEN

When I woke again, I realized Zephyr was moving around on the mountain.

What's wrong? I asked, getting to my feet and almost knocking Sen to the floor. The small dryad had been sleeping until I moved.

They're trying to catch me again. They've got nets and something that looks like a cattle prod combined with a taser.

I guess they have not realized those don't hurt you.

The nets would make it difficult to move, though.

Worth flying away for a while? I asked, worried about him. If they caught him as well, this could get a whole lot worse.

Maybe. But I want to know how they keep getting up here. They don't climb the whole mountain, which means there's a door.

I blinked, Zephyr's words leading to lots of thoughts. My mind struggled to keep up. It was a way out.

Or a way for me to get in and help get you out, Zephyr added.

It was something we'd need to worry about a bit at a time. If they were trying to capture him, he had to evade them. The rest could wait.

Before sleeping, I'd thought of as many questions as I could to ask Cherisse today and at the same time felt for the elements around me, pushing farther out from where I was.

Again, I'd found that the elements beyond a certain distance felt uncontrolled, as if the elves couldn't reach that far. I also noticed that the elements closer felt different somehow, as if they'd been shaped. I didn't know how they fit my mind in the same way I did freer particles.

On top of that, I had finally detected the change in guards and the way one relinquished control of the elements for a small window before another elf of each element stepped in and took control.

Interestingly, they felt almost identical in the way they were controlling the elements. When I'd been in the warehouse and training other elves, I'd sometimes been able to tell who was controlling it, their feel different. These elves felt like they were the same person.

Or possibly they'd adapted their control. If this was somewhere this group had been hiding for centuries, if not millennia, it was possible the elements of the mountain and everything within it were making it harder on them, having changed the way Cherisse had explained. But if they had learned to adapt to a degree, did that mean I could?

Could a person shape their control to match the signature of past elves? Because if so, it could lead to all sorts of things, including that the dark elf my ancestors had captured might have got free and grown more powerful.

Zephyr seemed to lunge and moved away from me rapidly. I heard a faint dragon roar, the sound coming from out on the mountain.

What happened? I asked, worry filling me.

Don't worry. I gave some elves a fright, he replied, laughter in his voice.

I exhaled, more than relieved to hear it. This whole little adventure had been hell, and I had been on edge since the first elf had attacked me, not to mention finding out that Chris had betrayed us. All in all, it was easily the worst situation we'd been in, but I had to find a way out of it.

We're making progress, Zephyr said. He was still moving around but slowly, as if he were creeping. *Keep distracting them, and we'll do what we can.*

The words helped, and Zephyr sent a wave of warmth and optimism with them. Admittedly, he wasn't the person who had been starved and locked within a mountain for the best part of two days. I couldn't remember ever being so hungry, and my head was hurting once more.

I needed to persuade Cherisse I was almost there and see what else we could get out of her.

Banging on the door, I decided to try to buy Zephyr a reprieve. I called for the guards to fetch Cherisse so we could talk more.

If they heard me, they didn't respond, but it wasn't long before the door opened again. Cherisse came in, wearing a similar robe, but underneath she had on a dress of a different color, the hem a light green that suited her.

"Ready to open a portal?" she asked by way of a greeting.

I was pretty sure I looked like crap, my hair in need of a wash, let alone the rest of me, and every bit of me aching from sleeping on a cold hard floor. I'd slept in some crazy places with Zephyr and in dives while homeless, but never alone on a hard floor.

"Firstly, call off the goons on the mountain. They're in danger of getting eaten," I replied, ignoring her question and commanding her as if I were the one in charge and had every reason to expect she'd obey.

"He'd kill them?" she asked, studying me.

"Probably not, but he's been up on that mountain for almost two days, and he can get pretty cranky. We once dropped an agent off the side of the building for pissing us off. I'm pretty sure he'd be considering seeing if any of the elves know how to fly as well. The air elementals might survive that, but the others..."

My voice trailed off and I deliberately tried to sound bored as if I didn't care.

"Humans aren't elves," she replied, almost spitting the first word. "Being willing to kill one or the other isn't comparable."

"Not to you, maybe. But to us? They were attacking us with nets and weapons, and so are the elves up on the mountainside. As far as we're concerned, that's equally a problem."

It wasn't a lie, and Cherisse seemed to realize that. She stepped back a pace and nodded at one of my two guards. A moment later they were gone, and I told Zephyr I was pretty sure the elves were about to be called off.

"Now," I said, fixing my eyes on Cherisse again, "I have more questions. We might want to get comfy again."

She gritted her teeth, but I remained calm and impassive. This had to work, but I wasn't going to beg for information. I was powerful, and she needed Zephyr and me; that much was clear. We needed her to give us a chance to learn more.

Eventually, she nodded.

"This is the last time. If you don't gain enough information to satisfy yourselves this time, I will consider you hostile to our plans and desires and act accordingly," she said as she stepped away from the door so I could leave.

"Understood. I'll make sure I ask everything I need to," I replied as I strode out, leaving Sen to run along the ground, hoping the different view would make it easier for her to spot something.

Once again, no one paid much attention to her. I talked while we walked, commenting on the large number of cells lining the hallway.

"Like any society, we have rules and a code of conduct considered fitting for elves and the other mythical races of the order. If someone breaks those rules, they are held accountable."

I chose not to say anything, not sure I agreed with Cherisse's idea of holding someone to account but aware that arguing was probably not worth my time. In the end, I simply followed her to the elevator.

"So, ask me some of these questions," she said as we rode along.

My brain froze and I worried that I wasn't going to

think of anything to ask her, but then I remembered the first question I'd decided on the night before.

"How many elves were trapped on the other side? Elves have never seemed as numerous as humans, but you've implied there are a lot more over there."

"I cannot say for sure. It could be billions by now, much as it is here."

"This planet can't sustain that many humans, let alone all the elves as well."

"Could it not if elves controlled the Earth and cultivated the fields?" Cherisse looked smug as she spoke these words.

I had to fight not to roll my eyes. If the elves took that much control and there were as many, they would have the same problem here in no time. Eventually, all the elements would be uncontrollable, elves would get weaker, and everyone would starve together.

It wasn't a solution. Of course, I couldn't say that out loud. Instead, I nodded as if this hadn't occurred to me and moved on to my next question. As we got off the elevator on the library floor, I requested water again, then continued asking my questions as we walked down the hallway. This time, as soon as our guard left to get water, Sen slid out of sight, tucking herself in the nearest room so neither guard would notice she wasn't with me anymore.

Distracted by what Sen could see, I almost stumbled over the threshold of the library room. I managed to cover it and walked to a table, where I sat down.

Cherisse fetched several books in the attempt to give me the information I sought. I did my best to appear as if this were slowly having an effect over the course of the day.

Sen found several possible routes out, her view a distraction I didn't pay attention to. She snuck into the room as I finished the first jug of water and asked for another.

"I'm not sure you need any more," Cherisse said.

"A little for Sen, then," I said as she slipped between the legs of the guards and into the room, her reconnaissance done.

Cherisse frowned and was about to shake her head when I scooped Sen up from the floor and placed her on the table. The little myconid tilted her head to one side and practically fluttered her eyes at the strict elf. That was enough to make her cave, although she rolled her eyes as she did.

"Very well, but the next time, you will offer your creature a drink the first time you are brought one. I won't allow more in future."

"Noted," I replied before I asked if it might be easier to break the pillars keeping anyone from getting close to the portal if someone had all four of the items the great elves had possessed.

She raised her eyebrows, something she did when she hadn't expected the question I'd asked. I waited for her to consider it but hoped she wouldn't take too long. While I wanted to pretend I was considering my options and trying to be cooperative, it was tiring.

"I don't think so. But if it were possible, we'd need to find the other two. I believe the whereabouts of the others are unknown."

I nodded, not intending to tell her that one of the Sanctuary elves was confident they could find the water elf's ring—not that he'd known it was a ring he was looking for the last time I had talked to him about it.

"If I could find the other two?" I asked, my mind offering me a possible solution.

"Then you would have to tell us where they are, and we would go get them," she replied without missing a beat. "I'm not that foolish."

"That's not what I meant, but I understand." I sighed before moving on to the next question.

Learning as much as I could and buying Sen more time to look around, I asked all the questions I'd planned, plus extras I thought of along the way. I could tell near the end that Cherisse was growing impatient with me and was beginning to suspect these were not real objections.

"Right," she said as she snapped the last book shut. "I think that is enough for now. I understand your reluctance, and I appreciate that we're asking a lot of you, but it's time to decide. Will you help us willingly, or do I have to be more persuasive?"

"Interesting way of phrasing it," I replied, stalling for time while I tried to think of the best way to say no that wouldn't anger her, or how to delay answering. "I'm going to need to talk to Zephyr some more. What you're asking is very dangerous and I still have reservations. It's clear you have a much greater understanding of this than anyone else I've met."

"None of which answers my question," Cherisse snapped.

"Not exactly, no. I don't want to declare I'll do something I can't and get your hopes up, but you've made me see things from a different perspective, and I don't want to refuse you. I'm considering it, but I won't promise something I can't be sure we can deliver. Is that an answer you'll accept for now?"

Cherisse's eyes narrowed as she studied me. I tried to appear calm, knowing I was asking her to hold off yet again.

"You've got an hour," she replied. "Then you'll be taken to your cell."

"Naturally." I fought not to roll my eyes at her over-bearing and controlling manner. She might have an advantage, but my powers were regenerating, and I wanted to give myself as much chance as possible.

I think we're going to have to make a move soon, Zephyr said.

Yeah, I can't stall anymore.

Under the watchful gaze of three elves, I picked Sen up and tucked her into the top of my jacket. Then I was marched through the building and into the elevator.

I think I've found where they go in and out.

Up on the mountain?

Yeah. It's a small hole. I'd have to take human form.

Then not yet. We'll get Sen out and give her time to get help.

Zephyr growled in response; it wasn't what he wanted, but I was worried that if we tried too soon, it wasn't going to work. And I wanted Sen safe since I was all that was protecting her.

They needed Zephyr and me. They didn't need the myconid.

CHAPTER EIGHTEEN

The hour passed too quickly, but we didn't waste it, instead hatching our plan to get Sen out and coming up with several contingencies to make sure it worked no matter what Cherisse tried to do.

We couldn't cover every angle, and there was a chance this was going to get Zephyr or me killed, and possibly Sen too, but the alternative was risking killing the entire planet for this mad sect of elves to attempt reuniting with a group that might or might not be friendly.

I couldn't do what they asked, but I had to make it look as if I would attempt to.

When the hour was up, I didn't need to bang on the door to get Cherisse to come back. She did it on her own, flinging the door open while I was going over the last of the plan and Sen was tucking herself into my jacket pocket.

Cherisse looked me over as I stood.

"Well?" she demanded.

"I'm going to need your strongest fire elf," I replied. I

wanted to indicate that I intended to attempt to help when it was all a bluff and another stall for time.

As I spoke, I could feel Zephyr moving farther away, making his way closer to the portal and the glass panels on the side of the mountain near it. He would watch what happened from a safe distance, ready to try to help me if I needed it. I hoped I wouldn't, but we weren't going to take the chance.

Cherisse frowned in response to my statement, but she nodded and waved for me to follow her.

I had no doubt we were heading to the portal as we stepped into the elevator.

"Have Phyrus summoned," Cherisse said as we reached the floor full of glass.

An elf I'd not noticed when I was up there who was standing in a small alcove to one side of the elevator nodded and ran off.

Cherisse didn't stop to check that the elf had heard her, instead striding toward the portal. It felt as if it took longer to get there this time, but I could soon see the strange area, and nerves ran through me. It was going to be hard to get this part right.

"Where's the dragon?" Cherisse asked a moment later.

"Nearby," I replied as I stepped to the boundary of the forcefield the pillars were creating.

"He'll need to be closer."

"No, he won't," I replied. "I'm attempting this, not him."

"That's not what we agreed," Cherisse said, growling the last word.

"We didn't agree to anything. You admitted I could

attempt it, though it would be harder. I'm not putting his life in danger if I don't need to. He's the only dragon left."

Cherisse looked as if she might argue, but an elf wearing a matching robe strode up with a gnome I recognized. It was the guy who had stolen my hairbrush and been part of my capture. I scowled at him, having no intention of pretending I liked him.

"This is Phyrus. He's our most powerful fire elf."

"Good. You're going to stay safe yourself, but you're going to focus on putting the fire out inside me and keeping me at the right temperature, do you understand? This goes wrong and I die, it will be your fault. You got that?" I asked him.

He gulped but nodded, his eyes flicking to Cherisse and checking she was on board with this.

"I must admit, Henera, you've got balls to try this yourself when the dragon is safer," the gnome said.

"And you've got balls coming anywhere near me," I replied. "You'd best all stand back."

As I finished speaking, I took my jacket off and helped Sen sit on top of the piled-up material to one side of the area. She was out of sight, and I hoped she'd stay that way.

I then looked at Cherisse and the two guards blocking my way to the rest of the building.

"Am I right in thinking the three of you can control the other elements between you?" I asked.

"Yes," Cherisse replied for them. "We can. The same three elements you command."

"Good. I want you to help keep my body stable as well. I need to step into the very edge of the field these pillars create to do what I need. All of you can stay safe and fight its control over my body."

Cherisse nodded and motioned for the other two guards to step forward until the four elves were standing in a row behind me, the gnome pulling out a device from his jacket and coming a bit closer.

It looked as if he were going to monitor the situation, possibly able to detect the pillar's effect on the area.

You ready? I asked Zephyr and Sen.

I don't like this plan, but I'm as ready as I'm ever going to be to see you risk your life for something we don't want to do. Zephyr's deep voice came with a comforting warmth despite his disagreement. I appreciated it all the more, knowing he was there for me no matter what.

Sen ready, the dryad said, moving in the pile of jacket so she could get going as soon as I had everyone concentrating on me.

"Ready?" I asked the elves, looking at them.

"We're ready," Cherisse replied, her tone curt and implying the rest had better be ready or they would pay for it later.

It was all the reprieve I was going to get, and a moment later, I felt a strange tingle in my body as the elves prepared to take control of its elements. None of them connected yet, allowing me to do something similar, but it was strange having their reach and their minds inside my very person.

And this was where the trust began. I had them inside me. I didn't doubt that against all four of them, I would struggle to defend myself, especially since I couldn't yet control fire, if I ever would be able to.

Moving an inch closer to the barrier, I tried to calm my racing heart, but there was nothing for it. I was simply too nervous.

Now the real acting would begin.

Stepping a few inches closer, I felt the pillars try to tear me apart. All four elves worked to combat the pillars and keep me safe in a strange tug of war that stole my focus and made my whole body itch.

Focus, Zephyr said as Sen began her journey. *You need to reach for the pillars and step closer.*

Got it, I replied, keeping my focus on Zephyr's voice and the soothing emotions he was sending my way.

I briefly wondered how this must feel for Zephyr and Sen before I moved deeper. I was forced to work with the elves to keep the pillars from tearing my body apart. I had to let the other elves control parts of me while I wrestled the strange devices for control of the other parts of me.

It felt horrible but I could endure it, fighting the effects of the pillars and its attempt to control me as the other elves helped.

Slowly I reached out with my mind, finding the elements in the forcefield also fighting with me as I tried to reach out to a pillar.

If I had been in good shape, I'd have been able to batter my way through, but I wasn't, and I didn't know when I would lose my focus. Until I'd made it look as if I'd made a good attempt at fighting this thing, however, I had to keep going.

Trying not to break anything, I reached toward the nearest pillar, the one with the fire symbol etched on it. As I did, heat burned my stomach, and it began hurting.

"A little help," I said as I fought to get closer to the fire pillar.

"Doing the best I can," the fire elf replied, and the pain lessened for a moment.

"Hurry up and get this done," Cherisse commanded. I could hear the strain in her voice.

"Working as fast as I can," I replied. "I've never tried this before, and you've been starving me for days."

"Then get the dragon to do it, and we'll all help him."

I ignored her suggestion. There was no way I was putting Zephyr through this; that wasn't part of the plan.

How's it going, Sen? I asked her as I finally reached the pillar, feeling the rock resist my control more than the air in front of it did.

Sen almost out, she replied, her voice as cheerful as ever.

It was a relief, but I had to keep up this ruse. A dull throbbing was beginning in my head, however, the first warning sign that my abilities wouldn't hold up much longer.

I was pretty sure the other elementals were beginning to struggle as well since their efforts to protect me were getting sloppier. This wasn't going to last much longer, and whether I wanted to open the portal or not, it wasn't going to happen now.

Trying to work out what was powering the pillar, I explored it with my mind, grimacing as the pain in my head grew.

Sen's out. Get out of there, Zephyr said.

For a moment I kept exploring, finding there was a crystal in the center of the pillar. I knew I couldn't do more than find it, though. The pain grew as all of us exhausted ourselves.

I eased back, losing control of everything in front of me. At the same time, I faked more pain and whimpered. Not knowing whether they were buying it, I tried to make it look as if I were losing control of my body, forcing the other elves to protect more of me.

At the same time, I threw myself backward, trying to get out of the forcefield.

Instead of going down, hands grabbed me, holding me up and keeping me in there.

"Break one of those pillars *now!*" Cherisse yelled, but I didn't try, instead doing everything I could to keep myself alive. I closed my eyes and went limp.

A moment later, I heard a dragon's loud roar and felt him come closer. Glass broke nearby, but I tried not to react. My powers were gone, and my head was pounding so badly that I was feeling sick.

"Let her out." Zephyr roared so loudly that Cherisse winced and her hands slid on my back.

"Get in here and finish the job, or I'll keep her here." Cherisse almost screamed the words.

"Kill her, and I'll lose my bond and abilities," Zephyr countered.

For a moment, no one moved or did anything. I wanted to scream, but I was pretending to be unconscious as if the whole thing had taxed me far too much or something had ruptured somewhere.

I stayed limp until Cherisse caved and let me down out of the range of the pillar. I fought the urge to peek or react, letting my body fall where it did. I could hear the elves panting in the background as someone lowered me gently to the ground.

"I think she came close to getting the first pillar broken," the gnome said. "She was right. If we hadn't starved her, she might have managed to break at least one. It was an effective strategy."

Cherisse growled, and I heard something clatter. Elves were shouting and running. Zephyr moved away from me and flew into the air, the tug on our bond growing worse and making me sicker.

I'll return as soon as I've lost them. Then I need to find something to eat.

I wasn't going to argue. Zephyr keeping himself safe was a huge part of the plan. I was the one who had been captured, and I was going to need plenty of rest if I was going to get out of here.

I felt a gentle pair of hands reach under me. One of the burlier elves picked me up, another helping support my head until I was in his arms, my head against his shoulder.

"I'll take her to the cell. I don't think there's any permanent damage to her body," the elf said, his voice unfamiliar.

"Fine," Cherisse snapped, and a moment later, I felt someone drape my jacket over my stomach. No one seemed to notice that Sen wasn't with me since the myconid was often tucked out of sight or trailing along on the floor.

I could still about feel her nearby, and I reached out to her with my mind. A moment later, I watched as she floated along a stream as it bubbled down the outside of the mountain. She was making her way north, and I hoped she would find Minsheng and that being so far away from me didn't break our bond.

Slowly I was carried to the cell, pretending to be unconscious the whole way. I was worried they'd pick up on the ruse, but no one seemed to question it. I acted as If I were coming to not long after my bearer stepped out of the elevator.

I opened my eyes to find one of the guards carrying me. Both of the other elves were with me as I was borne along.

"She's alive. Can you hear us?" the other guard asked.

I nodded, wincing as pain flared in my head, the reaction genuine.

"Nice try at getting that pillar broken," Phyrus said. "I don't think I've ever seen anyone come so close."

"Thanks," I said, "But unless I get food or drink regularly, I'm not going to get any closer to achieving it. I wasn't anywhere near full strength."

I watched their eyes go wide and Phyrus' mouth fall open. They had clearly thought I had maxed myself out. The thought amused me, but I didn't show my reaction.

My body was beginning to recover, but I stayed passive, hoping to keep the respect and warmth from these three elves, if nothing else. They believed I was on their side and I was interested in helping them. Maybe they'd help me.

I was placed inside of my cell, the guards gentle. They backed up.

"I'll find you some food," Phyrus said. "And when everyone has had time to rest, we'll all try again if we have to do it a pillar at a time."

I nodded, not intending to argue as the three elves backed up and shut me in again.

As I watched them go, I almost felt sorry for them. They had no idea I didn't plan on helping them. They'd been brainwashed into thinking they were doing something great, but my pity only went so far.

The three of them were complicit in keeping me a prisoner, and they seemed to have no qualms with Cherisse forcing me to try if I refused. For that, I could never like them.

CHAPTER NINETEEN

It felt strange now Sen was long gone from my reach, and I couldn't feel her anymore. She had been part of my world for so long that I was used to her presence in my head and the way she moved and thought.

We'll find her again, Zephyr said. *No matter what happens, we'll meet up with her soon.*

I sighed and hoped Zephyr was right as I took another bite of the food I'd been brought. Zephyr had found some mountain goats to feast on and was sitting somewhere above me digesting them.

It was strange to think that three days ago, we'd been in the kitchen at the warehouse, chowing down on pizza. Now here I was, reduced to begging for food. Zephyr was hunting wild animals, and Sen was who knew where, trying to find Minsheng and the others.

All of them would be panicking about me, but I'd tried and failed to persuade Zephyr to fly off and find them. He wouldn't leave me, and I couldn't blame him.

If they come close, I'll know. I can direct them the rest of the way. I've made sure people have seen me. With any luck, the news will get to Erlan and Daisy that there's been a dragon sighted here. They'll come.

Zephyr had told me that more than once, and it comforted me, though not enough. I couldn't help but worry that the others wouldn't find us.

No matter what happened, I intended to try to rescue myself. Having eaten, I felt a lot better. My body was putting the calories to good use. It would take more to make me feel my fully powered self again, especially after extending myself, but it was progress.

At least Zephyr was well-rested and at full power. That was a bonus to our escape plans. In preparation for making an attempt, I reached out with my mind and tried to feel the elements around me. The elves nearby were controlling them all again, keeping the grip tight but not commanding any of it to do anything.

It was strange to be surrounded by it, but it was a clever trick. Trying to work out their control and see if there was a way I could inspect the elements for signs of being more attuned to one or another of the elves, I concentrated.

Air was where I started, although I did so carefully. Every particle in the cell felt as if it was locked down, but I noticed it all had the same pattern to it. Gently, I reached out into the corridor, trying to find air that wasn't controlled by anyone. It wasn't easy to do, but eventually I found an alcove full of air no one was controlling.

It had a similar signature, one that resisted my control when I tried the usual way to connect. It felt odd to reach out to it, but I didn't use brute force as I might have done in the past. If it was hard to control elements that others had long been attached to but the evil elf had once subdued everyone and posed so much of a threat, there must be a way to make it easier.

No sooner had I thought this than molded my connection into a different shape, changing the way I coaxed the element until it fitted to me as naturally as whoever had claimed it for so long they'd morphed it. It felt strange and drained me at first, but it grew easier the longer I did it, almost as if it were getting used to me as well.

Slowly I moved the air around, controlling it but being careful not to move it too far and butt up against something controlled by one of my guards.

Have you discovered how to get around the elves' biggest long-term problem? Zephyr asked.

I'm not sure, I replied, barely daring to breathe.

Had I?

There's a marker on any element that has been controlled by others for a long time. I molded my connection around it.

I don't think most elves know how to mold their connection. You just connect. We just connect.

Before today I did, yeah, I replied, feeling smug. It seemed I *had* worked out a way around it.

But why hadn't anyone else? It didn't make sense. Was there a way I could get answers? Was it worth asking?

I had no idea, and I didn't have the brainpower to think about it much. We'd had a long day, and I had pushed myself hard. Although I was beginning to recover, I wasn't ready to draw attention to myself yet.

A couple of hours after I'd eaten, Zephyr moved again.

More elves out here, he explained. *I can't tell if they're looking for me or not.*

Stay safe, I replied, sitting up and reaching to control the air around me. I managed to stop myself in time, not wanting to alert the guards to my regained strength.

Not long after, Zephyr shifted to another section of the mountain, farther up where he could keep an eye on the elves but also blend into the dark of the mountain as the sun sank below the horizon. It made me feel more relaxed about his predicament, but the sound of footsteps in the corridor beyond caught my attention soon after.

Cherisse strode into my cell a moment later. She immediately spotted my empty plate and glared at the guards. No one spoke.

"I want you to try again," she said.

"I can't yet," I replied. "I've not rested enough."

"You've clearly been fed. You'll cooperate in this if you mean to help us, or get the dragon to do it." Cherisse strode forward as if she meant to haul me to my feet.

"I need more rest, and I've made it clear that I will be doing this, not Zephyr. Also, he's not *the dragon*. He has a name."

"Zephyr, then. But one of you is trying again right now."

"No, we're not," I said, getting to my feet before she could drag me. "I've said I'll help, but you're going to have to wait."

Cherisse frowned and let out a growl, but she backed off as if she might finally be accepting my insistence on resting more first. I was beginning to relax when she looked at my jacket and then around the room.

"Where's the dryad?" she demanded.

I didn't answer, looking around the room too as if I also didn't know.

"She went with me to try to open the portals. I left her on my jacket. Didn't she come back?" I asked.

"You don't know where she is?" Cherisse almost screamed the question.

"She doesn't stay by me all the time," I replied.

"I thought you were bonded."

I exhaled and nodded, pretty sure the game was up. This was about to go horribly wrong.

I'm coming, Zephyr said a fraction of a second later.

No, I thought back. *The point was to have everyone but me safe. If you come too close, you'll be in danger as well, and I don't want them forcing you to do anything.*

I can't stay up here and feel them hurt you.

They haven't...yet.

I looked at Cherisse, who had changed color, her face red and her fists clenched. So far she wasn't trying to do anything to me, but I expected it at any moment.

"You're not going to escape from here. You understand that, right? We outmatch you collectively, and this entire mountain is attuned to us. You'll help us or die here, and I don't care which." Cherisse stepped forward, raising her head and shoulders like an animal making a territorial threat display.

Deciding to meet her gaze, I stood firm.

"You can think what you like and try to make yourself

as intimidating as you like. Nothing has changed. Now, are you going to let me rest or not?"

Before I could react, Cherisse slapped me hard across the face. My head rocked back and to one side, but I managed to keep my feet and stop myself from striking her back.

"I'm growing tired of your insolence, child. You might not have had all the education one of the elves living here does, but you've been in contact with enough of us to know that when you're talking to an elder elf of pure heritage, you do so with respect. I won't make any more allowances."

I blinked, thinking the elf before me was insane, but I got the impression that antagonizing her further wouldn't be a wise move. Trying to get my body to relax, I stepped back. My cheek smarted where I'd been struck.

"Noted," I replied. "The elves at the Sanctuary think that with me being Henera and of pretty good pedigree, I was to be respected as well, but there are clearly differences between there and here. I'm used to being able to state when I've had enough and leaving it at that. I understand that you're eager, and it sounds like you and the other elves here have been waiting a long time for this opportunity. Alas, I need to ask you to wait one more day."

Cherisse stepped forward again and I felt the water in the rock move underfoot, almost making me fall over. I found my balance and reached for the water to take back control, pushing into hers, instinctively matching the glare she gave me.

Easy, Zephyr said, reminding me this wasn't how I was

supposed to be handling the situation. Once again I fought to calm myself and slowly relinquished control.

"I'm exhausted," I said, deflating as I did. "You can punish me or whatever you intend to do, and I won't be able to defend myself properly right now. But it's not going to make it any easier for me to get those portals open if we fight or you push me."

"I'm still not sure you are Henera," Cherisse replied, a sneer crossing her face. "You might be able to control three of the four elements, but you're far weaker than everyone thinks."

I simply waited. I was holding back, but having her underestimate me was exactly what I wanted, although I hadn't expected it to be so easy. When the time was right she would realize her mistake, but not before I was ready.

"Rest, then," she continued, turning on her heel but pausing at the door to look at me. "In the morning, you're going to break one of those pillars, or I am going to keep you in the field until you do or that dragon of yours does. Is that clear?"

"Entirely," I replied. It made one thing very clear: I had to escape before then.

Still not sure how to go about it, I sat down and let them shut me in the cell again, reaching out for Zephyr with my mind. His comfort and warmth washed over me, making me feel better instantly, but he was still on the move, and it tugged at my stomach.

The combination of fear about what would come if I didn't make it out of this place, the distance between Zephyr and me, and the loss of my connection with Sen was enough to make me sick. This was by far the worst situation I'd ever been in, and I had very few ways out.

I'm going to find a way to you, and then we're getting out of here, Zephyr said, the determination in his voice not masking the concern he felt.

You can't, I replied.

I have to. We need to work together, and you need to show me how to control the elements these elves have marked so deeply. If it's something the others can't do, it's the best advantage we have.

Although I wanted to fight Zephyr and insist he stay safe, part of me was desperate to have him near again. It was starting to tire me out, and on top of that, I missed the comfort he brought with him. I also didn't think he would let me convince him otherwise anymore. As much as I wanted to keep him safe, he desired to protect me, and right now, I was in danger.

With nothing else to do but wait for the right moment, and so as not to distract Zephyr while he was trying to find a way in, I sat down and closed my eyes, letting my body rest and recuperate. I was going to need every last bit of power I had.

I felt Zephyr come lower down the mountain and off to my left, his body moving in bursts as he followed something or someone the way a tiger might stalk its prey. I hoped he knew what he was doing, but with no way to get to him, I had to wait.

Eventually, he paused for a longer period and I reached out to him, wanting to check that he was fine.

Taking human form, he said a moment later. *Only way I can fit inside this place and come to you.*

I exhaled, desperately trying to keep myself calm and

not worry about him. We'd kept his human form secret, although Chris might have seen it, but that was about to end anyway. It was a shame, but I needed him, even though I wished I didn't.

As he started moving again, I followed him with my mind, getting glimpses of what he could see as he came closer. He was still outside on the mountain, snow covering the rocks and making them slippery. It was then that I realized how cold he was. Although he was hot-blooded and not like a reptile, he still needed warmth.

Before I could apologize for not being more observant about his situation, he followed the tail end of a group of elves as they came through a rock door. It was swinging shut as Zephyr slipped inside, his eyes adjusting far more quickly to the bright light inside than mine would have.

I almost cried out when he was spotted, the elf controlling the door having been on the other side of it seconds ago. Zephyr moved fast, grabbing the elf and shoving him while covering his mouth with a hand.

"Continue shutting the door," Zephyr said, his words coming out in his human voice yet still echoing in my head as if he'd spoken directly to me. The elf with him panicked and let out a muffled squeak as Zephyr applied pressure to something.

A moment later, the door swung shut slowly, and the cold wind from outside was gone. Zephyr never let his attention waver from the elf he had pinned, and as soon as the door was in place, he used his abilities to knock the poor guy out by hitting him over the head with a rock.

It would be much easier if I could use my breath weapon in human form, Zephyr said to me as the elf slumped to the floor. Zephyr stripped him of his robe.

I wanted to laugh, delighted he had gotten inside so quickly and easily. As he slipped the robe on, I reminded him to find somewhere to tie up the elf out of the way and gag him, then I exhaled.

Our escape had begun. Zephyr was on his way to me, and I was about to find out what I was truly capable of.

CHAPTER TWENTY

It didn't take Zephyr long to get the elf into a storeroom for dry goods down the next corridor. There was no sign of the rest of the elves who had come in off the mountain. All of them had gone deeper into the strange warren they called home.

Still, Zephyr planned to blend in, wearing one of their robes and doing his best to appear as if he were one of them.

I tensed as he tried to work out where the elevator was. Although he was closer to me than he had been in many days, he couldn't just walk to where he felt me to be. The elevator was some distance from my position, and each floor was different in its layout.

While he strode down hallways and passages, trying to work out if he was going in the right direction, I reached for the elements around me. I was going to have to find a way to get out to him and not rely entirely on him if this was to work. We needed to use our abilities equally. The last thing we wanted was for one of us to be drained and become a risk.

I could feel the control of the three elves who were guarding me. Two of them stood outside the door, the water and air under their control. I wasn't sure where the elf who controlled the water was or if it was Cherisse, although I knew she was capable of it, and she often did when close.

They were the unknown facets of this escape plan. I'd won over the earth and air elementals standing outside my door, and I'd seen the looks of pity on their faces as Cherisse had threatened me. I was pretty sure I had them to thank for the food I'd eaten.

Deciding to see if I could appeal to their softer hearts, I got up again and knocked on the door more gently than normal.

"I need the toilet," I said. "Can one of you escort me to one?"

There was no reply, so I repeated the question.

I waited, fairly sure I heard whispers as if they were talking about me and trying to keep it quiet. As Zephyr rounded a bend and found a group of elves dropping off nets and weapons I froze, my focus stolen by the threat this represented to him.

Not missing a beat, Zephyr strode closer as if he were supposed to be there.

"You all pulled the short straw again and had to go hunting on the surface, then," he said, his accent one I'd never heard him use. It sounded archaic and yet was very much how the elves spoke here.

I marveled at how well he could pull it off, but the elves studied him as if he didn't fit in.

"Haven't seen you around," one of them replied.

"I've been out on a mission. Gathering intel, but Cherisse said she had the dragon and his elf here and asked me to come back. What better way to catch a dragon than to have the elf who knows the most about dragons here to help? I'm sure we'll all get him next time."

I could hear the delight in Zephyr's voice as he pretended to be someone else, but I had to let our link go. The door to my cell swung open as Zephyr continued walking.

"We'll take you, but you need to be quick," the guard on the left said to me, his eyes shifting to the elevator as if he expected Cherisse to return at any moment and punish him for helping me.

"I'll cooperate," I said. "I want to get this all over and done with."

That relaxed the elves since they mistook my meaning. They thought I was talking about the pillars, not my captivity in their mountain. Slipping through the gap they'd left me, I walked out of my cell and let them follow as I strode toward the elevator.

Zephyr continued to make his way above me, the distance between us lessening as he mingled with elves. Some glanced his way but most ignored him, the robes making him blend in.

I tried not to show my fear for him as I turned the corner to face the elevator. I walked toward it with confidence but the swiftness that needing to relieve myself would create. At the same time, I reached for the elements, exploring who controlled what and feeling for free sections I could work with.

Neither elf I was with was making much of an effort to keep me encased from all sides in the air or earth they controlled, but whoever held the water was doing so for a considerable distance in every direction. It was strange, and it made me worried that there was someone far stronger than me here, at least in that one element.

No one is stronger than you. They're on their turf, as we've learned, but I think we can beat them, Zephyr said, finally coming in sight of the elevator on his floor. There was finally a break from other elves, and Zephyr relaxed since no one was looking his way.

Before the guards I was with could summon the elevator, Cherisse stepped out of it on Zephyr's floor, flanked by eight other elves.

Shitsticks, Zephyr said, echoing my sentiment.

I froze, terrified of what might happen but unable to get there fast enough.

Play weak. We'll find another way out, he said, but I wasn't sure I wanted to do so. As my oblivious guards summoned the elevator to my floor, I realized I couldn't without at least getting to Zephyr and finding out what the two of us were up against.

"So, you're the dragon in human form," Cherisse said, her eyes sweeping over Zephyr as I hurried into the elevator. It wasn't a polite look, and it made me angrier at her. For someone who wanted to be respected, she wasn't good at returning it.

As more elves surrounded Zephyr, the hope we'd escape fading from me. I jammed the button to go to the floor Zephyr was on as the guard I was with protested at the floor I chose.

"You'll understand when we're there," I said to him as Cherisse and her guards surrounded Zephyr. The guard offered no resistance, but I could see the desire in him to do so, coupled with anxiety.

The elevator couldn't move fast enough, every second agony since I knew any moment something could happen. Thankfully, the elevator doors opened on his floor a moment later, and I stepped out. The guards' mouths dropped open as they took in the sheer number of elves and what was happening.

Without hesitating, I hurried past Cherisse and straight into Zephyr's arms. We leaned our foreheads against each other as the centaurs did to greet one they cared about, and my stomach and his settled for the first time in ages.

"Are you all right?" he asked, not hiding his words from the others.

"I am now," I replied, also open about how much our bond meant to us. I had a feeling they knew, and I was too relieved to care.

"Well, isn't this touching?" Cherisse asked, sounding anything but touched. "You two reunited at last. Seems as if you're more than bonded as well. I had no idea an elf would sully her bloodline or the last dragon would consider his sole offspring being a mongrel, but I suppose that's what happens when an elf is raised in the human world."

I didn't reply to Cherisse's words, but anger boiled up inside me at the insults. I found myself grabbing control of all the air in the room and blasting it at her before anyone could react.

It knocked her off her feet, then four of the elves stepped forward. They took control of it again, and the floor grew less stable under our feet.

Zephyr's arms held me steady as he fought to control the section of rock we stood on, and I held a bubble of air tightly around us. It acted like a slipstream and stopped us from being knocked over that way.

In my mind, I showed Zephyr how I had molded my control and how it allowed me to grab on with more force than before, but neither of us pushed outward or did anything more than defend ourselves as Cherisse got to her feet.

"Stronger together. That is interesting, and you'll put it to good use. Bring them to the portal," Cherisse commanded.

The elves worked as one to use the elements and their physical bodies to herd Zephyr and me to the elevator, but we resisted for a moment.

We can't fight this, Zephyr said.

But we can't give in and break those pillars, I replied.

We need to look like we're too weak. You need to look like you're too weak.

Won't they make you?

No. Trust me.

It was all the encouragement I needed. I let go of the air holding us upright and pretended to faint again. Zephyr caught me but was knocked down before the elves around us realized something was different.

"She can't handle it, not until she has rested. You're

wasting my energy as well," Zephyr yelled, the growl only a dragon could produce clear in his words.

I moaned and leaned into Zephyr and he cradled me to him.

Cherisse yelled her frustration, the ground and the mountain trembling. Zephyr reached out and steadied us again.

"You have both of us where you want us, and there are enough of you that it's clear we have no choice, but I won't let you kill her out of haste or blindness to the truth. If you push us any harder, I will bring this mountain down around us rather than let you kill Aella for no good reason."

There was so much conviction in Zephyr's words that I was certain he meant them. My heart swelled, but I did my best to focus on the exhaustion I had to show.

"No. You will break one of those pillars, and you will do it right now. I don't need to kill your precious elf to remind you who is in charge here. Phyrus, make her burn," Cherisse commanded.

Phyrus stepped forward, but Zephyr got to his feet again with me in his arms and stared straight at the young elf.

"If you hurt Aella, it will lower the chance that I can break a pillar. And I *will* defend us and use up more of my power," he said calmly. "All of you want those pillars broken, don't you?"

Zephyr looked at the other elves, most of whom were nodding and staring, not sure what to do.

"Enough of this stupidity. We'll do it together, all of us, but not until we've all rested."

That broke their animosity, and I felt as if Zephyr had said the most amazing words and was convinced that was the plan for the moment. Before Cherisse could say anything else or command we do anything differently, he walked past her, pressing buttons on the elevator to take us to the floor with the cells.

Not a normal room? I asked.

No. They'll be more likely to let their guard down if we use a cell, and it will be us and the guards on the floor. If we claim a normal room, we're likely to be surrounded by elves when we want to escape.

Good point.

I sighed and rested my head on his shoulder, almost lightheaded at being close to him and beginning to come down from the adrenaline rush of the narrowly avoided fight and potential death of one or both of us.

Our life was nothing if not eventful.

Cherisse didn't follow, but several elves did, including the usual two. I didn't point out the futility of bothering to guard us. There wasn't a lot they could do against both of us in small groups, but we didn't want them to know that yet. For now, we were still making it seem as if we wanted to open the portals.

In minutes, we were in the cell together, entwined and resting. For what felt like ages and no time at all, I simply wrapped my arms around him and closed my eyes, enjoying having him there. He held me close and stroked my back.

You're thinner, he said. *I don't think they're feeding you enough. Next time we want to get away from LA, I think we should head to the Sanctuary, or maybe we should go to the UK for a holiday.*

Italy, I replied. *The home of the best pizza. And ice cream.*

Italy it is, then.

I chuckled, feeling better. It was as if having Zephyr here allowed my body to focus on regenerating and not maintaining the bond between us. We were stronger when side by side.

We dozed for hours. Neither of us slept, but we wanted the other elves to relax and assume we were resting as we'd said.

When the moment was right we would make our move, but not before we were ready. And not before I'd taught Zephyr what I was doing to connect to the elements around me.

Showing Zephyr how it felt to explore the elements around us and what about them was different helped me forget that we were in the middle of a mountain as prisoners. It was as if we were at the Sanctuary or the dojo and were having another lesson.

I'd have wished for more food and some water, but we were together and I was calm for the first time since we'd been taken. I wasn't alone anymore, and neither was Zephyr.

CHAPTER TWENTY-ONE

Zephyr took control of the rock in the mountain far below us and shifted it almost imperceptibly when he knew we were ready. We'd given ourselves the best advantage we could and made sure we had enough rest. If we left it much longer, the elves were going to start waking up, and then we would be up against everyone again.

It was time to escape.

Zephyr nodded at me, and we got up. Standing side by side, we reached for the elements and took control of them. We opened the door by pushing on the lock with air and shoving the guards as we did.

As soon as the door was open, I ran out and grabbed a guard. Zephyr seized the other.

"For what it's worth, I like you two," I said as I pinned my elf and glanced Zephyr's way to see him using similar martial arts on the other.

Their eyes went wide, but they didn't put up much of a fight as we pulled them into the cell. I didn't think it was going to hold them for long, but I wasn't sure what else to do with them.

Moving backward, I looked at Zephyr. He shrugged, and we simply closed the door, then he glanced at the other cells to see what held them shut. There was a padlock hanging on the handle of one of the other doors.

Might make it take longer for them to get out, Zephyr said as he added it to the cell door. Not inclined to argue, I hurried to the elevator. We needed to get out of here, but we didn't want to draw attention to the elevator moving. Instead of calling it to our floor, we pulled the doors open with our minds and revealed the shaft.

It was fairly dark inside, but we could see light leaking around the doors from each floor, so we could count the floors down and up.

Annoyingly, the elevator was down, stopping us from going all the way to the bottom and out of the mountain the way I'd come in, but up was also an option as well as back out the way Zephyr had entered. I couldn't work out how many floors were below us.

I don't know if I could take dragon form quickly enough if we get into trouble, Zephyr told me. *And it's cold out there otherwise.*

Frowning, I suggested we go down instead and get as low as we could before the elevator moved up again. Hopefully, we could bypass it when someone called it up.

It was the most dangerous part of the plan, the shaft a place in which we could both plunge to our deaths. The elevator could also crush us since the large object was able to move faster than we could get out of the way.

Still, it was our sole way out.

Taking a deep breath, I took control of the air around me and propelled myself into the space before letting myself drop in a controlled descent. Zephyr did the same, both of us taking extra care and not rushing given the extra difficulty of the marked elements. It wasn't as hard as it had been to control them, but it wasn't as easy as it was in LA.

We'd gone down about ten floors with the elevator still four or five below when I saw it wobble and heard the clatter of something inside it.

It's about to move, I said to Zephyr.

He flew over to the nearest door, and I propelled myself up to him to help him try to get it open before the elevator came up. We were still forcing the doors open when the elevator started moving, picking up speed as it came toward us.

Zephyr grabbed my arm and slipped through, pulling me after him so swiftly that we toppled over and landed in a heap on the floor. The hallway we found ourselves in was dimly lit and more roughly hewn from the rock. I assumed it was deliberate, given the style and opulence I'd seen everywhere else.

We looked around to make sure we were alone, but I heard voices approaching. I tried to find somewhere we could hide since the elevator was still moving and making noise behind us. There was an open doorway and we ducked through it, hoping the room would conceal us.

The longer we could go without someone finding out we had left our cell, the better. We had no intention of going back.

We ducked behind a table so we couldn't be seen from

the doorway as the footsteps came closer. They stopped near the doorway.

"Chris, was that you?" I heard the familiar gnome who'd started all this ask.

I hoped he wouldn't come any closer. We wanted to hide and stay out of the way, not get caught so soon. At least until the elevator stopped moving and we could get to the bottom floor.

Zephyr didn't let go of me. He was also doing his best to keep still and quiet, but I could see his gaze shifting as he looked toward the door and considered checking.

After a moment, the gnome came closer. I held my breath, terrified he would hear my heart as it hammered in my chest.

I knew we could deal with the gnome if we had to, but with every mythical we took out, we increased the chance that someone would notice we were at large.

To leave, we would have to sneak out. Cherisse had been right. Against a mountain full of elves, we weren't strong enough, not when it was harder to control the elements here for us than them.

As I was beginning to think discovery was inevitable and preparing to defend us, the gnome turned and walked out of the room, his receding footsteps letting us know we were alone once more.

I exhaled and relaxed in one motion, so relieved I was unable to move for several seconds.

Come on, Zephyr said. *Let's get moving again and hope we can get to the bottom.*

Without arguing, I got to my feet, and we hurried to the

doorway. We paused to check that the passage was clear before we moved toward the elevator.

The doors had shut, so we had to use both our hands and our magic to get it open and check where the elevator was.

This time it was a long way above us, so high that I could barely see it. Grateful for that, I took control of the air nearby, aware it was getting easier as I continued to adapt the connection process and work with what I had. Zephyr flew better, less wobbly as he joined me in the open air of the shaft.

Heading down, we both moved with haste, neither of us wanting to be here. It wasn't long until morning, when the elves would return to get us to break the binding pillars and open their portal. We had to be out of here by then.

We were a good portion of the way to the bottom when the elevator moved down again, coming down faster than we were flying. I glanced at Zephyr as he looked up.

When I went toward the nearest door to try to pry it open and get out of the way, Zephyr grabbed my hand.

No. We're almost there, and the odds are it's not coming all the way down. Keep going.

I wasn't sure I wanted to, but there was no time to debate. We dropped again, easing up on our control to drop faster.

My stomach tightened at how dangerous this was. We were in a barely lit elevator shaft, practically free-falling to the bottom of a mountain with the elevator coming down.

As we got closer to the bottom, I reached for the air to cushion us and slow us down. I was surprised to find it was easier to connect to here, the markers on it lighter and fresher.

I feel it too, Zephyr said. *I wonder if fresher air gets in here because of the doors to the outside?*

It was as good a guess as any and made sense. I was grateful, but we didn't have time to think about it. The elevator was still coming down.

The final door was way off the ground, so we couldn't land and try to pull it open. It was also stiffer, and I thought we were going to get squashed. I prepared to push against the elevator with all the air we were controlling.

It stopped three floors above us when the door was a bare two inches apart. For a moment, stunned and relieved, neither of us did any more. This was proving to be one of the tensest experiences of our lives.

By the time we were ready to focus on the door again, I could feel cold air coming through, fresh and almost unmarked. We had to be near an exit.

The thought filled us both with new energy and we pulled the door open farther, Zephyr using his dragon strength while I used my abilities to help. We slipped through as soon as the gap was wide enough, prepared to fight our way to the exit if we had to.

Zephyr took several steps before I had an idea. I reached for the rubber and chains that pulled the elevator up and down and tore them apart, slowly lowering the elevator to the bottom of the shaft. The weight brought it down on the springs that caught it in an emergency.

When I turned to Zephyr, I noticed the grin on his face. That would make it difficult for the elves to find us if they did realize we'd gone. Finally, we shut the doors to make it harder for everyone to work out where we'd got to.

With that done, I took stock of where we were. It wasn't the large garage-style room I'd been brought into but a massive storeroom. Closest to us were crates of foodstuffs.

Thanking whatever god or goddess was listening, I hurried over to one, and Zephyr helped me pull off the lid. It was full of savory snacks, the elves clearly having no problems with buying food the humans of this world mass-produced. We pulled off more lids, revealing everything from candy to trail mix to bags of flour.

Helping ourselves to anything we wanted, we stuffed our faces in a hiding place and then filled our pockets with more. At first my stomach objected to being plied with the strange assortment of foods and flavors, but the sickly feeling settled down as we worked our way around the room, following the very gentle draft with our abilities.

Instead of finding a way out, however, we found there were holes in the rock on one side of the mountain, the remnants of something once constructed of metal and woven into the very fabric of the mountain. The metal had rusted and corroded, and water and time must have then washed it away. Thin rusted metal pipes sat in discolored rock holes.

It was the source of the draft, but there was no way out for us.

What if we tunnel out? Zephyr asked. *We can control the earth and rock. It's possible.*

I don't think I could do it without drawing attention to it, I replied. *It would shake the mountain a bit, and even if we could mask that, it's a long way.*

Despite my words I reached out to feel the area around us and see if I could do something smaller or different.

If we were down in this storeroom for a while it might be possible, but we'd need longer than I think we'll have to do it carefully.

With nothing else to do for now, we kept exploring the floor. While it was expansive, the rest was more of the same: rows upon rows of food and supplies. We found water in bottles, the dust layered over them a sign that they hadn't been touched in a long time.

I wonder if they had a powerful water elf for a while or something? Zephyr suggested as he selected a couple of bottles and blew the dust off the tops.

After unscrewing one, he handed it to me. It was refreshing and tasted fine despite how long it must have been down here. It was also a comfort to know we were currently trapped in a place that could keep us alive for weeks if need be, perhaps months.

Not that I thought we had that long.

Up a floor or try to go through the wall? I asked Zephyr, feeling indecisive. This escape wasn't going badly, but I couldn't say it was going well either.

Zephyr didn't reply as we walked along the outer edge of the floor, going past the crates until we were at the source of the draft.

Stay here and see if you can make a way in for Sen. I'll go see if there's another good option.

I opened my mouth to object, but Zephyr was walking off, and I liked the idea of letting Sen come to us if we needed her. Of course, I hoped we wouldn't, but who knew how this was going to turn out? We were making up this escape plan as we went along.

Reaching out to the rock foundation of the mountain and the metal rods in the holes, I tried to figure out where to begin. I planned to work slowly and carefully and make sure there weren't many ripples of movement outward, but I soon found I wouldn't be able to work very fast anyway.

If the air down here was free from elven influence, the rock was the opposite, resistant to anything but the most exact molded control. I frowned as I tried to find the way it responded best.

This wasn't going to be easy.

Aella, Zephyr said a moment later.

What?

I don't think we'll be finding another way out of here. They've noticed we're gone.

Shitsticks.

CHAPTER TWENTY-TWO

Zephyr returned to my side and I continued to make the hole larger, deciding to remove the metal rod and then work with the rock. It wasn't easy, and that prevented me from going fast.

I tried not to worry about the elves who were looking for us. Hopefully, we wouldn't be easily found, but we were on a short clock. Once Zephyr reached me, he helped, also finding it difficult to connect to the rock but working on shifting it out of the way bit by bit.

Although I'd moved the foundations of the warehouse and rebuilt the walls from rock and stone, this was far harder. The mountain was made of something denser, and we really didn't want to draw attention to ourselves. If they worked out where we were swiftly, we were going to be in big trouble.

Neither of us spoke for some time. Zephyr occasionally looked at the elevator door to see if it opened or anything else happened in that direction. There were plenty of places we could hide down here, and I was pretty sure we could get out of sight before anyone appeared, but I didn't want to leave it until it was too late to move.

The hole was much wider, both of us working it toward the groove beside it when there was a noise from the elevator shaft. Without hesitation we hurried deeper into the storage area and down a row of crates stacked tall enough to shield us from both sides.

I took control of a small amount of the air and tried to determine what was happening to the elevator. I couldn't feel anything at first, but I kept my grip light and pulled it away from anything that might be the intrusive grip of another air elemental.

"This whole floor feels strange," someone declared, answering my question.

"Keep your voice down," a woman replied. It didn't sound like Cherisse, but we kept moving away from the voices and the sound of footsteps.

While we walked, Zephyr took control of the air around us to muffle any sounds we made and make sure we couldn't be heard despite being able to hear them. For what felt like ages, we moved from one row to another and up and down until we must have traversed the entire space at least once.

"They're not here," the first voice said. "We've been around the whole thing, I'm sure."

"What if they're listening in and avoiding us?" the woman snapped.

"We've been quiet for ages."

I had to fight not to laugh aloud. If the blundering around they'd been doing was their idea of quiet, I would be intrigued to find out what they were like when not being careful.

Zephyr rolled his eyes and led me around the next corner to put more distance between us and the other elves, but they either stopped or stopped making noise for a moment.

Fear crept into my stomach. Were they being quieter, or had they paused to listen?

Deciding not to stop in either case, Zephyr and I went down the next short row and into another, putting more distance between us and where the elves had last been.

We'd not gone far when I heard them speak again. They were farther away, and I had to stop and concentrate to hear what they were saying.

"You know, there's a chance they found the old staircase," the woman said a moment later. "I know they covered it with a thin layer of rock, but she's an earth elemental. She could have found it."

"They don't know to look for it," he replied. "And remember, the dragon can do everything she can while in dragon form."

"Yeah, apparently, but we've not seen it in action, and it's only a rumor. That gnome Cherisse is getting her information from might be wrong. They've been hiding his human form from everyone."

"And they're hiding from us. Cherisse is going to be shouting at us all morning."

"Come on. We'd best go report this floor clear. With any luck, we'll get assigned outside the mountain and won't hear her venting at everyone else. They've probably gotten away, and I don't want to be around when she realizes it," the woman said.

Zephyr and I crept down the next row, making sure we were out of the way as the two elves returned to the elevator shaft.

There's another way out, Zephyr said, giving me a grin.

A staircase, at least. Not necessarily a way out.

Possibly somewhere to hide until we can get out.

I chuckled as I thought about how we might be able to hide inside so well that they'd think we were out in the world and be looking for us in LA when we'd still be here.

The laughter died quickly, however. Neither of us wanted to remain here any longer than necessary. As one, we moved to the walls, but Zephyr encouraged me to return to the holes instead of looking for the stairwell they'd talked about and went off on his own.

In case we are in here a while and Sen returns to us, make the hole big enough that she can get through. But try to disguise it.

Zephyr didn't need to say anything else to encourage me. I wanted the three of us together, and I wanted us to be safe. The sooner we could achieve both, the better.

Now that we knew they thought we were elsewhere, I felt more relaxed, but I continued to keep an eye on the elevator. At some point they'd get it working again, which meant more elves could appear on the floor we were on even if they weren't looking for us.

Trying to work out the best way to hide the hole I was widening, I brought the rock I was moving slowly forward and curved it around and up so light didn't shine through it. It would make it harder for Sen to get through, but unless I had the time to make it bigger, it wasn't going to matter anyway.

I kept working, balancing being careful with movements I was making and the speed I was going at. When I began to tire, a headache forming, Zephyr exclaimed.

Found it? I asked.

I think so, he replied. *And I don't think this just goes up a few floors either. This...*

When his voice trailed off, I wanted to go to him to see what he'd found, but part of me still hoped Sen would return to us. I wasn't going to abandon that idea.

Keep going, Zephyr added a moment later. *I've got to make a hole big enough for us in here.*

It was a good point, and for the next hour or so, we kept working. I had to stop a couple of times and eat, grateful we had an almost endless supply, but eventually, I was done.

With Zephyr's help, we moved crates and covered the area, doing our best not to make it obvious. Finally, Zephyr led me to the hole he'd created in the wall.

My powers were almost depleted again, the marked earth having drained me far quicker than anything else had ever done, so I let Zephyr make the hole wider for us. Then we looked inside, having to crouch.

I saw we had a problem; there was no light inside the stairwell, and although we controlled three elements between us, we lacked the one we needed for this problem —fire.

We'll have to embrace the dark, Zephyr said. *We'll be together and in no hurry.*

I sighed as I looked up at him. Although I wasn't scared

of the dark, being in it for an unknown length of time filled me with dread. We had no idea what was in there except for the stairs. I could feel that the air went a long way up and expanded out, but we'd need our abilities to make progress.

All right, I said a moment later. *Let's go in and see what we find.*

Zephyr went first, the only one of us with much power left, but we barely made our way inside before he turned and looked around. We felt outward and found there was a wide space at the bottom of the stairs.

We should bring in plenty of food and water, Zephyr said.

It was a good point, but I was more than tired.

I'll do it, he offered, but I shook my head. We had only recently reunited, and I didn't like being apart from him at the best of times. We would get supplies together and hope we were putting energy into the right things.

It didn't take us long since there were plenty of crates of food to choose from, and we soon had a pile stashed to one side of the stairs. It almost seemed like overkill, given that we were trying to escape, not live here for weeks on end, but it was better to be prepared. Along the way, I'd also looked for a flashlight or matches, but didn't find either.

Time to hide and rest for a bit, Zephyr said as he followed me into the blocked-off stairwell. Turning to the hole we'd made, Zephyr activated his powers again and made the gap behind us smaller.

Leave a hole big enough for Sen, I said when he went to close it off.

For a moment he hesitated, but then he nodded and

made sure there was a gap she could fit through. It also gave us a small amount of light.

We both sat down and rested, the day having slipped by as we worked to keep ourselves hidden. Getting out definitely hadn't gone according to plan, but we were still together and alive, and we had finally some wiggle room.

I felt better about our future, but I wondered where Sen was and if she was safe. However, there was nothing I could do to help her. She was out in the world, and I had to have comfort in knowing that she had been for many years before we'd bonded. Of all of us, she was the oldest, but I had no idea how far she'd have to travel.

After a short while, Zephyr reached out to reassure and distract me. Trying not to think about it, I focused on him and my relief at having him close before we decided to get some sleep, opting for one to nap while the other kept an eye out.

It almost felt like old times when we were on the run, except instead of being in fields hiding in the crops under the sun, we were in a mountain hiding in the dark.

Once we'd both slept, we got to our feet, grabbed snacks and water, and prepared to explore our new area. After our rest, we could take control of the air again, although I noticed that it had a different marker and it was musty-smelling as if it didn't circulate much.

Using the air to guide us through the space, we climbed the steps in circles like the tower of an old castle but less narrow and tightly wound. At each landing, we found a thin wall between us and the inhabited area of the mountain. We stopped and listened at each one, trying to work out what lay on the other side.

At the first few everything was quiet, but at some of them we could clearly hear elves hunting for us. When close to those sections, we moved more quietly, but nothing kept us from climbing higher, and we continued to feel our way around.

We must have gone seven or eight floors up when we noticed an opening on the other side of the winding route. I moved toward it, feeling for the air and trying to see what it was and where it went. It sloped downward, but there was a hint of fresher air. I wanted to find out where it was coming from.

Zephyr took my hand as we made our way along it, both of us growing tired again. I hoped Sen found us help soon or we found a way out since I was exhausted, and it would only be a matter of time before the elves took more drastic measures to find us. I didn't dare hope they'd give up.

They're going to be very angry when they do find us, Zephyr pointed out as his hand squeezed mine.

Let's try to make sure that doesn't happen, I replied as I caught my foot on a lump of rock I'd not noticed and stumbled.

Zephyr steadied me, and we paused for a moment. This journey was taking its toll on both of us, wandering in the dark for what felt like hours, avoiding an enemy who would as likely kill us as capture us again and nothing easy to guide us to safety.

Grateful I had Zephyr, I leaned into him, resting my head on his shoulder. He kissed the top of my head and wrapped his arms around me.

This will all be over soon, and we'll be at the warehouse with the others. His voice was deep but gentle.

For a moment, I closed my eyes and imagined being with everyone, but it wasn't easy to do. They were far from here, and I was aware that if we got away from these elves and returned to our friends, our enemies weren't going to go away.

We'd made it clear we had the power between us to open their portal. They were going to hound us until we did so, and the thought terrified me.

After a short break during which I tried to think about happier times, we kept going, knowing we couldn't stop for long. We were far from safe, and that meant resting when we had to. The path wound back and forth and down, getting farther from the caves and our starting place as we descended.

For a while it seemed normal, but after a time, I was pretty sure I could hear something. However, the lack of noise and light might have been driving me crazy.

I hear it too, Zephyr said. Something was dripping and air was whistling through something, or water was rushing —a background white noise.

We tried to hurry, guiding each other and working our way down the slope in the rock. As we did, the passage twisted back and forth, the walls now rougher and closer in. At the same time, the air changed. I could feel water droplets in it, and there was a damp smell emanating from ahead.

As we rounded the next bend, I noticed the floor no longer sloped downwards. Water rippled over it.

The sea? Zephyr asked.

I blinked, but the movement made no difference to what I could see. However, the sound and feel of the water were unmistakable, the rush of the waves as they covered rocks and drained backward again. We had reached the ocean.

CHAPTER TWENTY-THREE

For a long time, neither Zephyr nor I wanted to move, the noise strange in our ears after being alone and in the dark for so long. It was also a relief to be in an area where the elements were no longer marked by this cult of elves.

I'd reached out with my mind, trying to work out if we could swim out of the cave this way, but despite the water coming in, I couldn't find a way to the outside with my mind. The tunnel before us was too full of water for as far as my abilities could go.

After hoping this might be an exit, it was yet another disappointment. I didn't move away from it, my mind still reaching. It was tiring me, but it wasn't until Zephyr pressed a candy bar into the palm of my hand so I'd take it from him that I realized I had another headache and must have entered a trance.

We'll find a way out, he said. *We won't be in here forever.*

I wasn't sure we would, but I didn't want to pour my despair onto Zephyr. Instead, I munched and tried to think of something else we could do. My abilities were drained again, but Zephyr had been more sensible and rested while I tried to find us a way out.

As soon as I'd eaten, he pulled me to my feet and slipped an arm around me.

I'll guide us while you regenerate. Then we can swap.

I wasn't going to argue, and I leaned into him as we slowly began the long climb toward the elves and the mountain caves they called home. As we did, tears trickled down my cheeks. This was almost more than I could handle. I wanted to be at the warehouse and safe, but once again, the abilities I'd never wanted had painted a target on my back.

Zephyr sent comfort my way, but he remained silent as well and wasn't feeling much better. These elves hadn't been kind about or to him either.

Part of me wants to open the portals, he said a moment later, in *the hope that there are other dragons.*

I'm sorry, I replied, not sure what else to say. I couldn't imagine being the last of my species, but I knew it couldn't be easy.

Every time I think about it, I come to the same conclusion, he continued. *It doesn't matter if there are other dragons in the world these portals connect to. I'm bonded with you, and I don't need anyone else.*

The words stunned me. I felt the same, but to hear that Zephyr felt it too and was willing to say it made me feel very different. I was his and he was mine, and nothing was going to change that. Not portals, not other mythicals, not anything else that was thrown at us.

With this thought we continued to climb, the return

journey feeling like it took less time than the exploration down.

We should rest and gather our strength to try to find a way out again, Zephyr said as we returned to our stash of food at the bottom of the stairs. It was easier to get back since both of us were getting better at connecting to the air and rock in the mountain.

We settled down, wrapping our arms around each other and trying to keep warm. The floor was cold, but it was better than it had been in my cell the two nights before.

We had dozed in and out for hours when we heard noises and voices coming from inside the storeroom. We sat up and listened, hoping to hear something useful.

The same two elves were back.

"I can't believe we're sweeping this place again," he said, his voice having a tinge of annoyance. "It's clear they're long gone."

"You've said that five times," the female elf replied.

I could imagine her rolling her eyes as they came closer.

"I mean, they fooled us all. Cherisse might be pissed off, but the last thing we all want to do is traipse up and down this place looking high and low when they're far more powerful than us and have escaped. I'm starting to understand why the humans are so scared of her and she does what she pleases all the time."

"Yeah. We knew the Henera would be powerful. I don't understand why Cherisse trusted her so much. I'd have had six guards there at all times and never fed her a single bite."

"Then she'd never have been able to open the portal," he replied. "We can't force her."

"Maybe not, but did you see the dragon's face when she

came to him? We need to torture her enough, and he'll do it. That dragon would die for her."

I tightened my arms around Zephyr as we listened, not enjoying hearing their opinions of us. It gave me hope that they believed we were gone, but I was still terrified of what might happen if we didn't get out and away from them soon.

They moved off, leaving us to try to rest more, but I couldn't go back to sleep after that. I was tired of the dark and cold. I wanted to get out of here.

We need to be careful, but I agree, Zephyr said as he stood and took my hands. *Let's get ourselves to the warehouse and our friends.*

I nodded, unable to speak as I thought of Sen and missed her little presence. I wanted her with me, and I was growing increasingly worried that she'd gotten lost or something had happened to her. If it had, I would hurt forever.

We'll find her, or she'll find us. I'm sure that as soon as we're out of this place, it'll be easier to find her. I'm pretty sure this makes it hard for our bond to be felt.

It gave me comfort, though I wasn't sure it was anything but wishful thinking. We ate something to keep our strength up and picked up more snacks to fill our pockets before we prepared to head into the dark once more.

Again we climbed, listening at the thin walls where we heard the elves. It was soon obvious that they were scouring the entire building once more, every thin wall offering a hive of activity and voices, although we couldn't make out what most of them were saying.

We seemed to climb for ages, always someone on the other side of the wall and too much activity for us to dare try to leave the stairwell. Once again we were tired, the climb and the constant need to control the air to feel where the walls were and what might obstruct our way in the dark draining us more swiftly than a usual day's activity.

I sat near the top as tears flowed down my face, and I let go of all the air to let my mind rest. Zephyr sat down with me and we cuddled, neither of us speaking.

We were there for some time while I calmed again. By the time I was ready to continue, there was a strange feeling in my stomach. I frowned and paused, holding onto Zephyr.

Then I was sure. It was Sen. I could feel her again.

Sen! I exclaimed, wanting to check it was her.

Sen back. Sen find help!

Her words were faint, but they were in my head. I felt better than I had in days, knowing she was coming with help. I almost didn't care who the help was. It was other people, and we were going to have a better chance to get out.

We should go down and meet her, Zephyr said, taking my hand. We rushed down, progress far easier although we were still tired. We stumbled and tripped several times, propping each other up to keep from falling while we hurried toward the small hole we'd left for the myconid.

On the way down, I directed Sen into the mountain and toward us. I could feel her get closer and closer as she came through the hole I'd made. She stopped near the end, checking for elves in the room and finding there were several.

This time they seemed to be trying to gather what stock they needed for the kitchens. She waited as we got closer and then we were at the bottom of the stairs, waiting for her and wondering when the coast would be clear.

Who came with you? I asked her as we were hiding.

Minsheng, Daisy. Others coming. Cranky lady getting help.

I didn't know who Sen meant until she sent me a picture of the woman from the organization. She had been irritated with us many times, but she'd also proven to be a useful ally when we'd needed one. If she was with us, we had more help than I'd dared to hope for.

Thankfully it wasn't long before the elves had everything they wanted and went away. The elevator appeared to work again. Sen came out of the long tunnel we'd made her and used her sense of where we were to make her way through the rows and stacks of crates.

When she burst through the small hole into the bottom of the stairwell to join us, I almost cried with relief and immediately cuddled her to me. For a moment, I basked in having the three of us together. It was exactly what I'd needed to give me hope again, but I knew it couldn't last.

We need to make a final plan and get out of here, Zephyr said, interrupting the moment but showering both of us with warmth and longing as if he were desperate to keep us together as well. With reluctance, I put Sen down again and told her what we knew and what the problem was, hoping she could tell the others what state we were in.

With that done, she ran off again, leaving the mountain the way she'd come. It hurt to have her put so much distance between us, but it was necessary, and we had to figure out a way to get the others in.

Sen managed to stay in range, her words sounding in my head as she told the others what she could. Her limited vocabulary soon ran out of ways to explain, but Minsheng picked her up to confer with the others, putting her on his shoulder.

Through her eyes, I could see Daisy, Erlan, Seth, and Ronan, as well as Gwaelon, Sierrathen, Ruehnar, and other elves I didn't recognize. Help had indeed come, and it almost made me cry.

To enable us to form a plan, Sen returned to us with a communication stone, one that would allow me to talk to Ronan. Relief flooded through me when she reached us, her path unhindered this time.

As soon as we were together again, I took the stone, and she hopped onto my shoulder. Zephyr came closer, intending to enter the strange void that allowed me to talk to Ronan.

At first nothing happened, but then I could feel my mind being pulled into the space where I could communicate with the centaur. Normally the room was dark until Ronan appeared and light along with him. This time, a strange sensation of being there and not quite there at the same time let me know something was different.

Ronan finally appeared, but he wasn't alone. Minsheng and Daisy were on either side of him.

The relief at seeing me in one piece was clear on Minsheng's face when he saw me. I tried to go to him, but I found I couldn't move. I was caught in one spot, the distance between us remaining constant.

I stopped trying, but it made my delight in seeing my friends bittersweet.

"We're here in mind," Ronan said, "but it is good to see you both again. Minsheng told the Sanctuary members what happened, and we agreed to help rescue you. Many of our elves are here. Sen informs us you are hiding but trapped inside the mountain."

"Yes," I replied, then told them as briefly as I could what had happened to us since we'd been taken. When I got to the part about the portals, Ronan interrupted.

"As much as we wish to hear the reason you were taken, this is best discussed in safety and comfort. Are you safe for now, and can we find a way to you?" The centaur spoke calmly and gently with no hint of reproach, only the desire to see us safe.

Again I almost cried with relief. We weren't alone anymore.

Taking a deep breath as I noticed Zephyr felt a similar emotion, I tried to think of what they needed to know and nothing more. I told them where I was and about the abandoned stairwell and the route that led to the sea.

We talked for some time, Sierrathen joining us as we plotted a strategy for escape and how to deal with the elves who would inevitably try to stop us. Although I wasn't sure what threats the mountain contained, we gave them an estimate of the numbers and what we would be up against.

Minsheng, Ronan, and Sierrathen took the news calmly, but they grew more serious. The forces we faced were the largest and most powerful yet, but we had the advantage of knowing a battle was coming. Only so many could get down to the lower levels of the mountain at once, the elevator being their sole route.

We went over our plan, its central focus being to get us

out and to safety without anyone dying or killing any of the other elves. The secondary goal was to find out if Cherisse would see sense and realize she couldn't open these portals.

I doubted the latter was possible, but Sierrathen was here as the Sanctuary council representative. I wasn't going to prevent her from attempting a diplomatic option.

Finally, we agreed about what to do and when, and it was simply a matter of preparing.

Although I didn't want to end the centaur equivalent of a video call, I had no control of it and soon found myself in the dark stairwell with the slight light from the hole into the storage room to see by.

Zephyr smiled at me, and Sen hugged me and patted his shoulder before darting through the hole. She left the stone with me in case I needed it again, but I was under strict orders to destroy it rather than let the elves take it if this went wrong.

Feeling more positive than I had in days, I sat down beside Zephyr to rest and wait for the signal from Sen.

CHAPTER TWENTY-FOUR

There was a lot to organize and not a lot for Zephyr and me to do while it happened. We munched on snacks, keeping the link open to Sen despite her being at the edge of our bond. I could see her on Minsheng's shoulder as he went over details of the plan with Sierrathen, Ronan, and Gwaelon.

When they were happy with their end of things, Minsheng, Sierrathen, and Daisy made their way inside the armored car they must have traveled in, taking Sen with them. I got to my feet, ready to get on with our end of the deal.

Everyone else split into two groups and flanked the mountain's main entrance, one group near the stairs by us, taking all the earth elves with them. They were going to try to make another way out if everything went wrong, while the other group would provide reinforcements to Minsheng should he need them.

Zephyr and I climbed the stairs until we were on the same level as everyone else and moved to the section of wall that led into a room. Although we had no way of being sure this was the level with the exit, it was the most likely and we planned to begin here.

I tried to stay calm, but I was more than nervous as we located the thinnest part of the wall adjacent to the next room and took control of the rock to pull it open.

It was time to get out of here.

With Zephyr beside me, we tried to power forward, not being quite as subtle but trying to keep the vibrations to a minimum. It wasn't ideal, but Minsheng had driven the truck closer and been greeted by four elven guards, so I wanted to make sure we were ready to intervene in case they needed help.

"We're here to talk to Cherisse," Minsheng said. "We understand she runs this group of elves, and we have much to discuss with her. I believe Chris the half-gnome is also here."

The elves looked at each other, not expecting something like this, but they didn't lash out or tell Minsheng and the others to go away. Thankfully, they'd hidden Sen, keeping her safe and out of the way until I was ready to make my move.

Ideally, we wanted some allies in here with us. If anyone was threatened, we planned to break through the sliver of rock currently hiding us, but unless the second group could break through and provide us with another way to get out, this was the best option.

"Go get Chris, or let us wait for Cherisse. I don't care which you do, but hurry up. We've come a long way, and we know you've recently had Aella and Zephyr here."

Minsheng folded his arms across his chest and tried to look as if he were in charge of the situation.

It was enough to get the elves to do something. One of them ran off as if he were going to fetch either Chris or Cherisse.

"Are the rest of you going to stand there all day?" Minsheng asked when the other three didn't move but continued to block the path. "Or are you going to let us park inside and out of this wind?"

The elves didn't react at first, just looked at each other. One of them shrugged, then they got out of the way and opened the gate wider.

I watched Minsheng drive in and I relaxed when I heard the hum of the motor on the other side of the wall.

Making sure our control on the wall was firm, we waited for Minsheng and the others to get the car in position. As soon as he was parked in a way that allowed him to drive right out again, there was a pause. The car continued to run, and it took all my self-control not to push out of the stairwell and run for the vehicle.

That wasn't the plan, however.

We waited, listening, the rock thin enough to hear as someone got out of the vehicle. Then the elevator doors swished open and someone came onto the floor.

"Chris," Minsheng said, "It's good to see you, although I never thought we'd be meeting like this."

"I'm not surprised you're here, but you've come sooner than I thought you'd be. Did that dryad of hers lead you here?" Chris asked.

Minsheng didn't respond and I almost broke the rock,

but the waves of calm coming from Zephyr kept me from doing that.

"I hope you didn't hurt her," my Shishou asked, the threat obvious. Sen shifted as he spoke, still hiding but giving me a better view through her eyes.

"I've not done anything, but she's not here. Not anymore. Cherisse is out looking for her, so if you think you'll get to speak to her, you'll have to wait, I'm afraid."

"What do you mean, she's not here?"

"Turns out she's a lot further from the sweet innocent elf on the run than we ever believed possible. She's a liar and was willing to risk the lives of others to benefit herself. Of course, it wasn't going to be long before she picked that up from the Sanctuary elves."

I saw Sierrathen step forward, only to be stopped by Minsheng. She looked as if she might smack Chris or use her abilities to do so, something I'd never seen from her before. It didn't look as if Minsheng were any less angry.

"Aella might not be perfect, but she is trying to do what's best for every race on this planet," Minsheng replied. "Not that I expect you to understand that. I won't say it again. We want Aella and Zephyr, and I want your promise to leave them and Sen alone in the future."

There was another pause, and again I almost broke through. As I gritted my teeth, my heart pounded in my chest, but I kept still and quiet.

"I can't promise anything. Cherisse runs everything here, and I assure you, she's not the kind to take threats lightly, nor betrayal. But come, we'll take you somewhere you can wait for her."

Minsheng backed up, shaking his head.

"No. We'll wait outside for Cherisse. You can let us know when she's back."

"It wasn't a request," Chris said as the elves came forward. I could both see and feel them preparing to attack, control of the air and earth under their feet crawling outward at a surprising speed.

Minsheng and the few mythicals with him would be overwhelmed in minutes without our help. We couldn't hide any longer.

As one, Zephyr and I broke the thin layer of rock in front of us, sending the brittle shards flying outward. They destroyed the side of the van I'd been brought here in, blasting holes through the metalwork and deep into the engine and interior and popping the tires.

I blinked, my eyes taking several seconds to adjust. Zephyr grabbed my hand a moment later.

The elves' mouths fell open as Zephyr and I ran for the armored vehicle our friends were beside, hoping we could drive off before the elves could react. We didn't get more than halfway there before one of the elves stepped forward and flooded the vehicle with water. It spluttered and died, the engine drowning.

I growled my frustration and grabbed control of all the water before hurling it at the elf and sweeping her off her feet with it. At the same time, Zephyr blasted another off his feet with a jet of air.

More elves appeared as Zephyr and I backed toward the door with Sierrathen, Minsheng, Daisy, and Sen rushing to our sides. Sen bounded onto my shoulder, the small myconid holding on tight as I rocked from a blast of air that was supposed to knock me off my feet.

Although I was running low on power and was tired, Zephyr and I didn't stop throwing everything we had at the elves, blocking the elements they threw at us, dousing fires with water, and keeping the floor steady under our feet of us and those of our allies. At the same time, we used the air to tear apart anything else thrown at us or knock it off-course.

The longer it went on, all of us inching backward, the more elves poured from inside the mountain, coming down the elevator in groups to reinforce the attackers with painful efficiency.

We were clearly at a disadvantage, the air, earth, and water in here so marked by their control that Zephyr and I alone were managing to hurl it back with any speed or skill.

Thankfully our reinforcements finally made it to us. One group rushed through the rock opening we'd left, having tunneled into the abandoned section we'd been hiding in. The others broke through the door behind us, tearing it off its rock-reinforced hinges and leaving a gaping hole.

We spread out, retreating as a group while trying not to kill anyone but putting up a fight until we were out in the open. Relief swept through me as sunlight met my face for the first time in three days.

A moment later, another blast of air almost bowled me over. Zephyr threw up a wall of his own and steadied me with a hand. Despite the extra elves with us, we were still hard-pressed. No one gave up and let us flee.

With the other elves lending their strength and power and all of us working our way to freedom, the task grew easier, however. Out here, the air was fresh and the ground unmarked, so we could find a better way to move.

Despite all that, it was clear the elves we were fighting had trained for situations like this. They worked in groups, never fighting for control of the elements between them, and each group worked as a wider unit. While several of them defended the elves as a whole, most of them targeted Zephyr and me, clearly trying to stop us from getting away.

Before long, all the elves on our side formed a circle around us, Ronan giving commands as he and the centaurs with him joined the fray. Unable to control the elements, they were using projectiles and slings, the contents cracking open and swirling smoke into the air when they landed.

I grabbed the vapor and pushed it where it needed to go, hoping it would obscure the space between the groups and help us get away.

Slowly, we moved back and back, gaining the upper hand as Zephyr prepared to take dragon form again, finally having the space. Before we got much farther, however, the ground shook beneath us, control of it snatched by a powerful elf.

Cherisse's voice rang out. "Give us the elf and her dragon." I whirled to see her standing behind us. Many elves stood with her, blocking our escape.

Shitsticks, I thought. Zephyr let out a deep rumble as he leaped into the air, blasting upward before wings sprouted from his back and he transformed.

Although I'd seen him change form before, no one else had, and there were gasps. The fight stopped for a moment.

It was clear many of the elves had never seen a dragon, let alone such a large one flying right above their heads.

"We aren't yours to claim," Zephyr yelled, his voice rumbling across the mountain's surface.

Without warning, he exhaled, gas coming out in wave after wave. I grinned, taking control of it and spreading it over the elves. Some of them fought back, blasting it out of the way with streams of air or fighting me for control of it.

I put everything I had into wrapping it around their heads, which forced them to breathe it in. Looking for Cherisse, I tried to get it to her, but like the mythicals had formed up around Zephyr and me, the elves she commanded did the same for her, protecting her.

The ground rippled underfoot as an elf beside Cherisse tried to pay us back. I saw the sea in the distance rise, but I pushed up off the ground and stabilized those around me.

Fly up, Zephyr said.

I can't leave the others. She'll kill them.

They'll focus on us.

I hesitated, not wanting to leave Minsheng, Ronan, and the Sanctuary elves behind, but Zephyr had a point. In the end, Cherisse made the decision for me. A wave of water rushed through the air and the earth elf near her hurled rocks at Zephyr. He was forced up and the elves were forced away from us by the jet.

Exposed, I had to blast up into the air, heading toward Zephyr until we met. Grabbing on, I propelled us higher.

We need to get everyone else out of here. If Cherisse realizes we're safe, she'll turn on them.

I know, but they can't reach as far as we can.

I could have smacked myself for not remembering that

advantage as Zephyr circled and we looked for an opening to attack. About a fifth of the elves with Cherisse were out cold thanks to Zephyr's breath weapon, but the rest were still fighting.

Exhale again, I told Zephyr.

He flew over them as he breathed out and I took control, pushing the cloud lower and wrapping it around any elf I could see who was controlling the earth. More of them went down before the air elves could stop me.

It was enough of a reprieve that Minsheng and the centaurs ushered some of the elves away from the battle.

Can we push them inside the mountain? I asked Zephyr.

I tried to figure out if it was possible. At the moment, Cherisse and her group were blocking the exit, and they were keeping anyone but us and any air elves who could fly from escaping.

We were so high in the air we were mostly being ignored, but I didn't expect that to last. We weren't the sole air elves in the battle, and I was pretty sure these elves had been trained to fight me.

Confirming my suspicions, a strong-looking male rose, pushing up with the air and calling to others to join him. Exhausted, I felt fear grip my stomach. We were going to struggle to get away from this many elves.

They're not as practiced as you, and they don't have a dragon. I won't let you fall, Zephyr said.

Taking a deep breath, I focused.

We weren't defeated yet.

CHAPTER TWENTY-FIVE

For a moment, Zephyr, Sen, and I flew higher, wearing the other air elementals out as they fought to catch up with us. I rested, not helping Zephyr as I kept an eye on the determined squad of elves.

At the highest altitude Zephyr dared go, I shivered in the cold air. The mountain had been warmer than this, but I knew we needed the disadvantage the height gave the elves.

As soon as Zephyr was blasted with air from the front elf, forcing him to roll to one side to save his wings, I reached out and pulled the control out from all the elves at the same time.

They fell for seconds as I used the air I controlled to blast them farther down. Some of them recovered quicker than others, but they were soon out of my reach and regrouping. Zephyr circled toward the mountain, trying to find an updraft that would make it harder for them to attack us.

I used the reprieve to check on the elves below, but the

battle was still raging down there. Part of me felt bad for leaving the rest of the elves to fight without us, but we'd taken a significant portion of the air elementals with us, and it appeared to be helping our elves regroup and press the advantage.

This time when the air elves came at us, they split into five pairs that came at us from different angles and heights. I wasn't going to be able to blast them to gain another respite.

Focusing again, I did my best to take control of the air around several pairs at once, knocking two of them back. The third was ready for me, and we wrestled for control for a moment before a blast from elsewhere almost knocked me off Zephyr's back.

He banked in the direction I'd been hit, responding to me slipping and giving me a moment to take control of the air around myself and get back into place. As I recovered, I hit the nearest elf with a jet of air and sent him spiraling away.

No sooner had I sent him packing than I was pressed against Zephyr by a blast from above. For a moment, I couldn't move or look around, the pressure too great. Once again Zephyr banked and turned, the blast sliding past us as he climbed.

The blond elf in charge stared at me, intense concentration on his face. This was the elf I needed to beat. The rest of the elves in the air with us were almost a distraction.

Want me to keep you close to him? Zephyr asked.

Yeah, keep him where I can hit him easily and try to avoid the others.

As he tried to throw more air at me, Zephyr banked

again but continued to rise. The elf didn't hesitate to follow us. I grabbed control of another chunk of air as it flowed over us and hurled it at the elf. It made him roll to one side, and I grabbed the air he was trying to control.

He fell, and Zephyr dove after him. I kept reaching for the air, sending the elf spiraling and spinning. At the same time, several of the others tried to come to his rescue, but we were falling faster than we'd flown up, and few of them could keep up.

I blasted another couple of elves away as they tried to unseat me and make it harder for Zephyr to fly. It gave our main target enough time to recover and he came up to meet us, hitting me in the face with a blast.

It was my turn to tumble, Zephyr unable to fly in reverse to prevent me from falling. Sen came with me, the myconid squealing in fright but holding on tight enough that I didn't lose her.

I panicked, fear gripping me before I could grab enough of the air to slow down. I spun as I slowed, and another jet of air knocked me off-course. All the air elves in the sky focused on me while I tumbled.

Outnumbered, I had little choice but to keep going down and try to keep the others at a distance while I hit them with everything I could. My head was throbbing and my powers showed signs of fading, and Zephyr was too far away to rescue me if I dropped from this height.

Distract them as long as you can, Zephyr said. *Then land.*

I wasn't going to argue or bother pointing out I hadn't been distracting them so far but fighting for my life. Instead, I darted to one side and hit three of them with air hard enough that they flew toward the mountain.

One landed with far less grace than I'd have expected and didn't take to the air again. Another went to their aid. That left eight in the sky with me, but before I could do more than dodge the commanding elf's next blast, Zephyr appeared.

The elves had forgotten about him, and he exhaled right in their faces. Several of them sucked it in without thinking and began falling, and the rest caught them—with one exception. The commander tried to duck. I flew at him, colliding and grappling and bringing some of the gas downward at the same time.

Taking a deep breath at the last moment, I enveloped us in gas, still clinging to the elf as he tried to push and kick me away. He inhaled before I did and went limp, falling from my grasp as I blasted the gas away. Too late to avoid taking in some myself, I grew lightheaded.

Zephyr, help, I thought as we fell, my control of the air no longer working well enough to keep me flying or catch him again. My limbs grew heavier, and my eyes tried to close.

Fight it, Zephyr said as I saw his bronze scales come closer.

I tried to do as he commanded by breathing in large gulps of fresh air. Then he was there, the last of my control enough to push me up and onto his back. I clung to him as he caught the falling elf and continued downward.

Land in front of Cherisse, I said as my head cleared. Zephyr's gas had worked through my system quicker than I'd have thought possible.

Zephyr didn't need any more encouragement as he flew toward the mountain and the elves who had come to aid us. As he landed and put the air elf he'd saved down, I reached into the ground with my mind.

This far out, the ground was clean and easy to latch onto, but I was at the end of my abilities, my head throbbing and my legs like jelly beneath me. This was the last task I was going to be able to perform with what strength I had left. If this didn't get us out of here, I was going to become a captive once more.

With all the strength I could muster, I made the ground ripple out from where I was in a semicircle that knocked a considerable number of the elves off their feet and made Cherisse wobble before the earth elf beside her took control and settled the ground.

Gwaelon seized that moment to unleash a torrent of water, the sea rushing out of the tunnels in the stairwell area. Three water elves with him helped him guide it onto the right path and it knocked over more of the elves, sweeping Cherisse back several feet. Once again she steadied herself, the water her element. She took over the blast, though Gwaelon fought hard.

As one, Ronan commanded all our mythicals to form up around me again, the air elementals taking the lead and buffeting those standing too close out of the way. It was the final push we needed, and they broke through the cult forces and came to us. I noticed some of them were limping and supported by others, but all of them were alive and determined.

For a moment I couldn't speak or move, the support all the mythicals had shown me overwhelming me. In every battle before now, we had fought side by side to rescue others or defend our homes. This time, they'd all come to rescue me from our own kind.

It meant much more, especially from the Sanctuary, who hadn't always agreed with what I'd done or my reasons. I had nothing left to give, however, the exhaustion from being on the run for so many days having taken its toll.

Despite that, I held my ground, not moving until every elf was safely through the group on the mountain. Then Zephyr strode forward, focusing on Cherisse. The elf we'd plucked from the sky was still in his grasp.

When we got to the front of the group, Zephyr gently rolled the air elemental forward. There was a stunned silence as I sat up tall on Zephyr's back and used what air power remained to float the elf to Cherisse's feet, trying to make it look as if it were easier than it felt.

If I was going to bluff, I needed to sell this.

"Going to surrender so we let your friends go?" Cherisse asked, her eyes mocking.

"No," I replied. "I'll never surrender or give you what you want."

"Then I will take it. You have no right to deny us a connection with our homeland." She stepped forward as if to attack, trying to spur her elves on, but many were as spent as I was, and others were still knocked out.

I felt and heard rather than saw the elves with me take a step forward, then I could feel their control in the air as someone put a wall around me.

"And you have no right to dictate this choice for everyone on this planet," I continued. "I know you want to be reunited with your families. I know you want to go home. But there's a good chance there's danger on the other side of that portal, and I won't make that decision for all the people on this side. No one should alone."

Silence met my words, and I didn't give Cherisse another chance to try to push me or take me back.

Placing one hand on Zephyr's shoulder as if it were a signal, I motioned for everyone to head toward the vehicles they'd traveled in. Zephyr led the procession, his head held high while I rested on his back, grateful the air elves with us were doing everything they could to make it appear as if I were still controlling it.

I didn't glance at Cherisse. Instead, I stared at the elves Zephyr was approaching. They looked as if they might win the most intimidating game of chicken I'd ever been involved in, but eventually, one took a step back.

It started a chain reaction, and the line broke.

Cherisse yelled for them to stop us, but the rest of them knew they were beaten and gave way. We walked through without looking back, and I remained where I was. Zephyr turned so we appeared to guard everyone as they entered the vehicles.

A moment later, I heard Cherisse growl and saw a funnel of water form, but Gwaelon immediately blasted it apart with water he controlled. She didn't dare try again and resorted to glaring at us from the middle of her cult.

When we were sure everyone was safe, the convoy rumbled away. Zephyr took to the air, flying above them all.

The elves never came closer, and as we left, they went inside. I finally dared to look, my eyes meeting Cherisse's as she stood at the entrance to the mountain.

I shuddered, unable to help it. For the first time in a long time, I'd walked away the victor out of pure luck. I wasn't strong enough, not to face elves as determined and ruthless as Cherisse.

We will be strong enough next time, Zephyr said. The words were a growl, determined and angry.

Next time. Yes, there was going to be a next time.

CHAPTER TWENTY-SIX

Zephyr flew after the vehicles for a couple of hours with Sen and me on his back. Several times I had to fight off sleep. The exhaustion I felt was so overwhelming I was sure I'd sleep for days when we finally got the chance.

We weren't safe yet, still in a different country with the locals not welcoming the sight of a dragon flying through their sky. It made me wonder what it had been like for Zephyr on the way here. He'd never left my side.

I flew a lot higher up, Zephyr replied as I finished the thought. *I didn't want the elves to get any ideas or the locals to get involved and risk making it worse.*

It made sense, and I was grateful Zephyr had been so careful. It also made me aware of how self-focused I'd been throughout this ordeal. Being trapped and taken and separated from Zephyr and Sen had made it hard for me to focus on all three of us.

They were putting you in danger to force my hand. I was never in need of your concern. It was right you focused on your-

self, Zephyr said. *It worked, and it got us out of there. But I'm never going to be apart from you again.*

The determination to see it be true rippled through me in waves, emanating from Zephyr with such force I couldn't do anything but feel it too. It washed away my guilt and helped me settle, comforted by being with him out in the open.

After being trapped for so long, it felt more than welcome to be flying, as tired as we both were. I was out in the sunlight and Sen made sure she was on my shoulder, enjoying the day and the breeze that blew over us.

For a while I simply reveled in it, watching the scenery change underneath us as we found ourselves in the country to get away from people.

It seemed to take no time at all to reach the border, our convoy having to slow and to stop as the officials manning the road grew concerned.

Zephyr landed and I slid off his back to act as our emissary, Sen still on my shoulder.

"We're sorry to approach you like this," I said. "I hope we haven't scared any of you. I was recently kidnapped and brought into your country, and my friends and family rescued me. We would like to return to our country, but we don't have our passports or anything."

The guard blinked at me, clearly having no clue how to respond, although I saw him glance a couple of times at Zephyr with one hand on the end of the rifle slung about his neck.

Before I could say anything else, Minsheng got out and came up beside me holding out paperwork of some kind.

"This is an emergency diplomatic visa covering

everyone with us, including Aella here, the dryad on her shoulder, and the dragon behind us. We'd like to return to the US. Our purpose here is concluded."

The guard studied the paper in front of him, then looked at Zephyr and me.

"Are you the elf with the dragon we've all been hearing about?" he asked as he held out the paper to Minsheng, looking at me the whole time.

I nodded.

"Could I get your autograph?"

It was my turn to blink. People had asked for my autograph before, but never like this or with as big a grin on their face. I heard Zephyr chuckle as he strode closer, lowering his head to appear less intimidating.

"My wife will never believe me unless I have something to prove I met you," he added, his hands shaking.

Zephyr lowered his head farther as Minsheng found a pen and handed me a scrap of paper. On autopilot, I asked the guard his name and scrawled a quick message before signing it.

Before I could hand it over, Sen ran down to the ground and stuck her hand in the dirt, then pressed her twig-like hand to the piece of paper to mark it with her handprint.

The guard's grin grew broader, then more guards came out of the hut nearby carrying more paper and motioning to Zephyr as well. For the next ten minutes, we signed autographs, Zephyr and Sen adding claw and handprints in lieu of their names and the other mythicals waiting.

I feel bad about everyone having to wait for us, but this was the kindest reception I could have hoped for after all the animosity, and I was grateful no one else was challenging us.

The guards finally noticed everyone waiting and offered to let the rest of the convoy through.

"I'll meet you at the Sanctuary," I told Minsheng and let him hurry the others on.

He hesitated, wondering if it was safe, but Cherisse had made no attempt to follow us, and I was with an array of armed guards. I couldn't be safer.

Part of me wanted to rush away with Zephyr and Sen, but I had wanted to have humans react this way to the presence of mythicals for so long that I was determined to show our best side while I could.

Once Minsheng was behind the wheel, the convoy wound its way through the gate and up the road. I watched them go for a moment before Zephyr pointed out that we could take the scenic route and follow the coast instead of the roads they had to follow.

I wobbled on my feet as I handed an autographed sheet of paper to the guards, who realized I wasn't okay.

"I've not eaten properly in about four days," I said when they showed concern. "I was a prisoner."

A guard hurried off to the hut and came out with something in a brown paper bag.

"Here, my wife always packs me extra sandwiches in case I do a double shift. Sounds like you need them more than I do."

I took the offered food with tears in my eyes at his kindness. It was quickly followed by all the others adding something to the growing pile in my arms. I thanked them all, feeding Zephyr some as I munched.

Beginning to feel more like myself again, I flopped down by the side of the road and had an impromptu picnic with the guards who weren't needed to man the border, grateful for something so innocent while I rested and recovered some more.

As soon as we'd eaten, however, Zephyr encouraged us to continue, and I said goodbye. Sen gave each of the guards a high five, making them all grin again, then I climbed onto Zephyr's back.

Although I could use my powers now, I was aware I'd been using them a lot, so I chose to chill and relax on Zephyr's back, the conversation having taken a mental toll of its own.

To the coast? he asked.

Yes, I want to be by the sea and away from everyone.

Zephyr leaped into the air as he unfurled his wings. Each powerful downbeat took us up until we could see the glittering blue of the Pacific Ocean, getting closer to it but also farther up the coast.

I gazed at it, grateful for the wide expanse and how I could feel the element so much better now. As we got closer, Zephyr descended and soared over the waves.

It was beautiful and made my heart lighter. We were free once more, each minute taking us farther from those who'd tried to force us to doom the world.

Grateful for everything that had led to our rescue, I reached out with my powers, marveling at how much easier everything was to control out here. It was another kind of freedom I'd missed.

While I was stretching into the sea, feeling the water

move and roll with my head, I noticed life in the waves—something strange, unlike a fish.

Circle back, I said to Zephyr as we flew onward. I lost it.

Back? he asked, although he did as I asked despite the question.

I felt something strange. Like a creature, but not one normal to this world.

A mythical?

I think so, I said. He circled as I searched the water.

It didn't take long for me to feel it again, a horse-like shape playing in the waves as they came into shore and rolled out again. Lower and lower Zephyr went until I could see it. There was a horse, almost translucent and appearing to be shaped from the water, with two beautiful foam-like wings sprouting from its back.

A water pegasus, Zephyr explained.

He's stunning, I replied as Zephyr landed on the shore not far from him, for it was a male.

Then he noticed us and ran out of the water, lifting his head and prancing in a happy greeting. I reached out to him with my mind, feeling the water that made up the majority of his body.

When he was still several feet away, there was a brilliant blue flash of light. Suddenly my mind was full of emotion, joy, warmth, and excitement flooding into my senses, along with strange thought-like words that rushed past like water in a river.

I stepped forward and the creature did the same until I could reach out and touch him, running a hand down his long, glistening head. He was warm to the touch and as smooth as silk, and my fingers sent out faint ripples across his skin.

He harrumphed like a horse, but I knew he was far more intelligent.

"Aella," I said, putting the other hand on my heart.

Roth, he replied, surprising me. Then he looked at Sen and Zephyr on the beach beside me. Both of them introduced themselves by name.

There was silence as all of us took in what had happened. Our bonded group of three had become four, this pegasus as much ours as we were his.

Drawn to him, I stroked his side, marveling at the strong horse shape and what he was made of before focusing on the wings he possessed as he unfurled them.

Can you fly? I asked, projecting it into his head.

Yes, as well as Zephyr can, although not as fast nor with as much skill. Dragons truly are masters of the skies.

As the pegasus is master of the sea, Zephyr replied, lowering his head in what passed as a bow.

I felt a hint of trepidation as they assessed each other, but there seemed to be a lot of respect between them.

How is this possible? the pegasus asked me a moment later. *You are bonded with all of us. Elves usually form only one bond.*

Yes. I command three of the elements, and it would seem I have a bond to go with each.

Roth dipped his head before looking at me again.

Then you are Henera, and I have been given an honor far greater than any pegasus before me. As he spoke these words, he lowered his head in a bow.

I blinked, surprised by how much he knew about me and the ways of elves.

My kind live a long time, and we talk to the elves and other animals when we can.

I worried that I was pulling another wonderful creature into my mess of a life. I could feel the light-hearted joy inside him, and I didn't want to taint it.

Don't fear for me, he said, making it clear he could feel and interpret my emotions. *I choose to come with you, no matter the danger and the end we come to. Any mythical who understood you and your destiny would.*

I nodded and bowed back, awed by the trust this creature had in me and the warmth in his emotions. Roth turned to Zephyr and bowed to him as well, and my heart swelled. My family had grown larger, and I was excited by what it meant for the future.

Before I could suggest we make our way to the Sanctuary, Sen jumped down from my shoulders and bounded onto Roth's back. Mirth rolled off him, making Sen and me chuckle in delight.

After I once more positioned myself on Zephyr's back, I poured warmth into him as well, wanting to make sure he knew the deep love I had for him was unchanged by this development.

Without a single one of us needing to speak, Roth and Zephyr rose into the air. Sunlight glistened off Roth's water mane and Zephyr's scales as we flew to the Sanctuary.

I was pretty sure I grinned the whole way, happy for the first time in days. There might be another threat in our future, and we had no promise of permanent safety, but with each day, week, and month that passed, we grew stronger and gained allies. If Cherisse thought she could bully us into doing something we didn't want to, she was going to be severely disappointed.

As we approached the Sanctuary, we flew lower. I explained to Roth that there was a shield that hid it from view, preparing him to be amazed. He flew down cautiously after us, Sen guiding him until he came through and the buildings, gardens, and elven habitat were revealed to his eyes, complete with all the mythicals who lived there.

Shock flowed through our connection, followed by delight, apprehension, and excitement. A whirlwind of emotions flowed from one to the next and back, and it took my breath away to experience it as well as everything going on inside me.

It was clear that where Zephyr's thoughts and mind melded with mine and Sen could give me her sight, my bond with Roth was on an emotional level.

He landed beside Zephyr, and I dismounted as familiar faces came out to greet us. Minsheng was the first to notice the pegasus with me, and he grinned.

"Does this mean what I think it does?" he asked as he came forward.

"Minsheng, meet Roth. Roth, meet my Shishou. He's my mentor, my friend, and the person who reports our where-abouts and progress to the organization," I said by way of a reply.

Roth bowed once more but didn't speak. I didn't know if he could.

Within a minute, Gwaelon appeared, with Ruehnar not

far behind him. They marveled at Roth, then introduced themselves. Gwaelon looked at me.

"I found it," he said with no explanation, then held up a ring. "I had to visit some elves in Europe where Ornthalas was rumored to have gone to rest in his final days. But I'm very sure this belongs to you, my dear."

Before I could react, he took my hand and slipped the band onto a finger. It was too large until he let go of it, then it shrank and fused to my skin.

I gasped, recognizing it as the ring in Cherisse's pictures. I could now feel much more water, and I was aware of not just the water but the emotional state of everyone around me as if it were in the liquid they were made up of.

"It seems it is time for another bonding ceremony," Ruehnar added. "Our Henera is truly among us."

EPILOGUE

I tried to keep calm as I floated beside Zephyr and Roth, Sen riding on Roth's back as she preferred to do now. The President had asked us to meet him at a mining location in the middle of Texas, requesting we come quickly and speak of it to no one.

Of course, we'd told Minsheng where we were going and why, but otherwise, we'd done as we were bid, pretty sure that getting a personal call from the leader of the country was a big enough deal to respond promptly.

As soon as we came into view, men came out to meet us and act as an honor guard. Before I could do more than nod at the man in charge of the unit, however, the President came out of a nearby tent and walked over to us.

"Thank you for coming, Aella, Zephyr, and Sen." The President gave his attention to Roth. "I don't believe we've met."

Roth bowed as I introduced them.

"Another bonded mythical?" the President asked.

"Yes. Shortly after I returned to the country, we found

each other along the Pacific Coast. Now that I can control three elements, I can bond with three mythicals."

"That's quite something, and I suppose that means we need to add Roth to our list of admittable folks." The President glanced at the aide beside him as he said this, and the man nodded and tapped on his phone. "I assume Roth is as sentient as your other mythicals."

"Yes," I replied. "Although he finds English hard to speak aloud."

"Fascinating. But please, let us head inside. I know you're a busy woman, and I understand you've had trials of your own recently. I must confess I was glad when your organization informed me you were safely in our country, especially when I was brought here to see this."

I lifted an eyebrow but didn't interrupt the President as he led the four of us inside the large open building that backed onto the mountain. We were led down a tall, wide hall that was barely big enough for Zephyr to fit through.

"The mine had to be shut down. They were drilling through to a large cavern they thought would open up more veins of ore and came across something unexpected."

Dread filled me at the President's words. I had a feeling I knew where this was going despite not yet seeing it.

"At first they thought they'd uncovered an old Native American ritual site, something they'd need to get an archaeologist for. But when they tried to get close..." The President shook his head, and his voice trailed off as he paused in front of a wide flap of plastic with warning signs all over it.

"It tore them apart," I finished for him, knowing what was on the other side.

"Yes. There are three dead miners and another who managed to back out of whatever...the field is around these pillars. He's in the hospital, and they have no idea if he'll recover or what could have caused burns inside of his body without damaging the outside."

I exhaled. "I know what this is."

The President nodded at the nearest security man, and he swept the plastic aside to reveal what I feared: another portal with the pillars that powered it. Farther out were the pillars that kept anyone from getting close enough to turn it on.

But this one was different. It was far larger, and it wasn't as dormant as the other had been. The air, earth, and moisture in the cavern hummed in the presence of the powerful pillars.

I stepped into the room as the President urged me to be careful. Reaching out with my mind, I stepped closer again, finding the edge of the zone the pillars controlled.

I had no doubt. This was the main portal to the elven homeworld, and I didn't believe it was a coincidence they'd found it now.

The story continues with *Day Sworn*, book 8 in the Dragon of Shadow and Air series.

Claim your copy today!

ACKNOWLEDGMENTS

Once again my publisher, LMBPN are making my dreams come true and being both lovely to work with and amazing at what they do with books. I am eternally grateful for everything you all do.

And a huge thank you to Bryan. Having you back in my world has made everything brighter and you inspire me to become more and believe more than ever. I couldn't ask for a better friend.

To my tiny humans, for teaching me that sometimes there's such a thing as too much curiosity and that sometimes we ought to be asking why.

To 4thewords and everyone on the team there. You have created this amazing writing place that helps me to keep coming back to write a bit more even on the hard days. I'm addicted to the, just one more little monster thing so much I must get so much more done per week thanks to your site.

To all my friends who put up with my ramblings, my

less than smart moments and are there for me no matter what.

Finally, to God, who somehow finds me that hidden path through all the obstacles.

ABOUT THE AUTHOR

Jess was born in the quaint village of Woodbridge in the UK, has spent some of her childhood in the States and now resides near the beautiful Roman city of Bath. She lives with her husband, Phil, her two tiny humans (one boy and one girl) and her very dapsy cat, Pleaides.

During her still relatively short life Jess has displayed an innate curiosity for learning new things and has therefore studied many subjects, from maths and the sciences, to history and drama. Jess now works full time as a writer and mummy, incorporating many of the subjects she has an interest in within her plots and characters.

When she's not busy with work and keeping her tiny humans alive she can often be found with friends, playing with miniature characters, dice and pieces of paper covered in funny stats and notes about fictional adventures her figures have been on.

You can find out more about the author and her upcoming projects by joining her on facebook, by watching her live D&D streams, or emailing her via books@jessmountifield.co.uk. Jess loves hearing from a happy fan so please do get in touch!

Jess is also opening up her discord for fans to come chat about what she's up to, and see a few sneak peaks of future work. There's also a chance to become one of her beta readers. If you'd like to check that out you can do so here.

CONNECT WITH JESS

Connect with Jess Mountifield

Mailing list sign up
Facebook group.
Discord group
Actual play D&D stream: Twitch or Youtube
Email address: contact me here.

Guild of the Eternal Flame:

Wayfarer's Sanctuary

Protector's Secret

Healer's Oath

Other Fantasy:

The Initiate (under Holly Lujah)

Writing with Dawn Chapman:

Jessica's Challenge (#5 in the Puatera Online series)

Dahlia's Shadow (#6 in the Puatera Online series)

Lila's Revenge (#7 in the Puatera Online series)

Sci-Fi:

Fringe Colonies:

Alliance

Haven

Rebellion

Rebirth

Reclamation

Star Trail:

Hunted

Sherdan series:

Sherdan's Prophecy

Sherdan's Legacy

Sherdan's Country

Sherdan's Road (A short story in the anthology 'The End of the Road')

The Slave Who'd Never Been Kissed (A short in the charity anthology 'Imaginings')

New Beginnings

Santa's Little Space Pirate

In the multi-author Adamanta series:

Episode 1 – Adamanta

Episode 3 – Excelsior

Episode 8 – Phoenix

Episode 13 – New Contacts

Episode 17 – Sacrifice

Other:

Clues, Claws and Christmas

Non-Fic:

How to Write Lots, and Get Sh*t Done: the Art of Not Being a Flake

Find purchase links here

Coming soon:

Urban Fantasy:

Dragon of Shadow and Air:

Water Bound

Day Sworn

Fantasy

(Tales of Ethanar):

The Pursuit of Winter (#2 in the Winter series, Tale 6.2)

Books under Amelia Price

Mycroft Holmes Adventures:

The Hundred Year Wait

The Unexpected Coincidence

The Invisible Amateur

The Female Charm

The Reluctant Knight

The Ambitious Orphan

The Unconventional Honeymoon Gift

The Family Reunion

The Immortal Problem

Coming soon:

The Unremarkable Assistant

www.ingramcontent.com/pod-product-compliance
Lightning Source LLC
Chambersburg PA
CBHW020405110726
47899CB00006B/1869